Before Kallen, there was Tarragon. Oryon history sees him as the first and greatest of all technomage kings. What history has forgotten, however, is that he was also the very first to partner with a symbiont.

At the age of eighteen, Tarragon becomes clan king by default. He alters the face of Oryon's history when he fully embraces magic and emerges as the first ever technomage king. Surrounded by deadly rivals who are intent on eradicating his family, Tarragon, as the last surviving heir, needs to learn how to control his magic and how to fight. Survival is not easy, and if it means getting involved in a dangerous secret, so be it.

Tarragon
Copyright © 2019 Jo Tannah
ISBN: 978-1-4874-2484-8
Cover art by Angela Waters

Published by eXtasy Books Inc or
Devine Destinies, an imprint of eXtasy Books Inc

Look for us online at:
www.eXtasybooks.com or www.devinedestinies.com

Tarragon
Rise of the Symbionts Book 4

By

Jo Tannah

"Name The One"

Name the one who established this colony.

Name the one who was chosen first among his kind.

Name the one whose partner sacrificed his life for the sake of the colony.

Name the one outsider.

Name the one who started the line.

Name The One.

CHAPTER ONE

Tarragon looked about him as he shuffled wearily over to where servants stood handing out the day's rations. The remains of the dead had been laid out and burned only that morning. Malcolm, the Guardian who had kept him safe for as long as he could remember, had not been among them. Tarragon had buried the man himself. He'd owed him that much, but he wished he could have done more. The fatalities from the battle the day before had been extensive, and morale was at an all-time low.

To boost lagging spirits and energize the exhausted bodies, there was nothing like a quick distribution of rations among his men. Thankfully, there was more than enough for every man. With the defeat of their enemies came the confiscation of the food supply. Even if the meals were cold, at least with their stomachs full, the Dacron soldiers would have something to prop their rapidly dropping energies.

When it was finally his turn, Tarragon only took a piece of bread and dried, salted meat. He stared at the bits in his hand, willing himself to find the strength to eat. His body ached, and he had no appetite to speak of, but he forced himself to take a bite and chew. He flinched when his teeth met the tough jerky. The painful throbbing in his jaw and the burning ache of swollen gums were incessant. Not to mention the wound in his leg and the one on his back.

In the end, Tarragon spat the morsels on the ground. When a servant passed him a waterskin, he drank from it in controlled gulps. Despite his aching thirst, he still had enough sense to remember that taking it all at once would only result in heaving and stomach cramps. With each gulp of warm water, his throat gradually felt less dry, though the back of his eyes were beginning to feel hotter. He wondered if he were getting a fever. As soon as thoughts of illness entered his thoughts, Tarragon took control of them. He thanked the Goddess above for giving him that ability, for if he did not, he would surely have crawled into someplace he wouldn't be found, curl up, and allow the shadows to take him to a gentler place.

Once more, Tarragon looked at the dead. At his estimation, more than four hundred of the soldiers who had served his family lay dead. By the sun's rising, more would perish. His soldiers were getting killed at a rate of five to one. Soon, his losses would turn critical until, inevitably, the enemy would rush through the barricades and slay them all. Tarragon concluded that despite their situation, his soldiers had surpassed his enemies' expectations. He looked about him with weary eyes and saw that some of the men were talking. Some were even laughing. He wished that he could talk to them about hope, but he knew he couldn't. Even if he could, he didn't doubt his men knew that their end would only be prolonged until dawn came. And then it would be all over.

Tarragon sat back against the rock wall. Its surface was an icy dampness on his back. Slowly, painfully, he removed his helm. He scraped back his soaked blond hair and reflected on his life.

His near-death exhaustion brought on one regret—that he would meet his death at only seventeen years. As the youngest son of a vain father, his service in the army had not been out of his free will, but in payment for his brothers' deaths. At the thought of his older brothers, he closed his eyes and willed away the sudden tears that flooded his eyes.

The first time he'd taken arms had been when his brothers

had taken him to the training grounds. That was on his fifteenth birthday, only two years before. Compared to his brothers and father, he had been small and short, but his brothers had all assured him that he would develop into his height. Just like they had. They hadn't lied. His muscles and strength had indeed caught up with his height, but none of his brothers had seen what they'd predicted. Soon after his fifteenth birthday, his father and brothers had left Tarragon back in Dacron Palace to attend the annual Oryon council of kings. That was when the dissenting clan, Zaruthra, had attacked, killing his brothers. They hadn't reached his father in time, though. His father had escaped with his Guardians. Seeing that his family had scrambled to defend themselves, another rebellious clan, the Caprici, had quickly joined forces with the Zaruthrans and taken advantage of the Dacron's momentary weakness.

Tarragon shook off the memories. Too late to wish for a better time while he was sitting here at his post. A piercing flash of pain from the wound in his leg reawakened his anger.

"Ahh, Goddess. Is it wrong to wish them all their deaths?" Tarragon muttered. When no answer from the deity came, he cursed at himself for acting the fool.

His leg throbbed painfully, and he couldn't contain the wince when he propped it out before him. Although the stab of agony racked through his body, he made no sound, lest the servants hear him and his father got hold of the information. The sun beat down relentlessly, and the weight of his armor pressed down upon him. The weakness he'd been ignoring for days overwhelmed him, and he knew his days were numbered. He looked down at the flesh around the puncture wound on his leg. The torn tissue was crusted with oozing, dark liquid. The throbbing continued unmercifully, and all he wanted to do was close his eyes and hope for the pain to ease. He raised his head at the blinding sky above him, the sounds of men in pain inside the medical pavilions dwindling around him. His circling thoughts drifted from the battle he'd fought only hours before to the days of fun and laughter with his brothers. There was no fight left in him as the aches from his injuries to those brought on by exhaustion overcame him.

The next thing Tarragon knew, someone was shaking his shoulder, and he jerked awake. Tarragon blinked away the gumminess on his eyelids and fought to clear his mind. He was young enough to have his senses come instantly on the alert. Without questioning why his rest had been disturbed, he started to rise, but the pain seared the length of his leg, causing him to gasp out for air. Thankfully, the soldier crouching low beside him didn't mention his momentarily lapse and instead offered a steadying hand. Tarragon took him to be older than him, but not by much. Like him, the soldier looked ragged and tired, but it was his eyes that caught Tarragon's interest. There was no pity in the violet depths, merely a steadfast resolve that offered Tarragon the support he desperately needed.

"Your Highness, the guards have reported that there are men coming up the hills. Just below the barricade." The man's deep-throated voice momentarily surprised Tarragon. He sounded older than he looked.

"Take me there," Tarragon said. He looked around him and saw the growing darkness around him. He scanned the sky, but could see no stars.

"Do you know what time it is?" Tarragon turned to look at the soldier and studied his face. The gaze the man returned had a penetrating look to them. Suddenly, Tarragon felt out of his depth. There was something compelling about the man, and he didn't know how to interpret his feelings.

The soldier turned away to frown at the sky. "I'd say it's

about sundown. You looked like you needed the rest, and I've been standing watch so you could sleep undisturbed, Your Highness. I'm sorry. I can't be more certain of the time."

Why did this man make him feel so uncertain all of a sudden? Feeling inexplicably challenged, Tarragon shrugged off his discomfort, forcing his voice to assume the tone of command.

"Take me to the engineers. We need to get those perimeter lights on before the sun sets. Hurry," he snapped out and immediately cursed himself. He didn't sound in command at all. Surreptitiously, he examined the man's face. The full beard and soot on his skin didn't detract from his attractiveness. Rather, it was as though the dirt and grime heightened his handsome features. And those violet eyes—they were stunning. So very different from his own blue ones.

He turned his attention once more to the problem at hand. Looking around him, seeing the darkness falling rapidly rather than the expected lights from the electrified perimeter fence that would keep their camp protected, he had no doubt that during the hours he'd been asleep, the Zaruthran and Caprici men had taken advantage of the falling darkness, encircled their camp, and flanked their position. He might be young, but two years of fighting the enemy had garnered him insight for their next moves. It was what had kept him and his company alive. Gritting his teeth against the pain in his leg as well as at the lack of perimeter lights, he allowed the soldier to help him get across to the other side of the camp where the corps of engineers was stationed. At least, what was left of them.

As he hobbled over them, the soldier beside him took in more of his weight. The support helped a lot, but it also showed his men his weakness. He straightened his back as they neared their destination, ignoring the searing pain shooting up his leg. He gritted his teeth and presented a mask of authority on his face. Tarragon looked at the individual faces of the engineers who stood to attention when they saw him approach them. There was a desperation in their expressions even though they were hurrying to do their assigned task.

"Report," Tarragon said, looking at one of the four engineers. One of the older men stepped up.

"We've worked all afternoon, Your Highness. But without the generators, there's nothing we can do to power up the lights and the fence. We're sorry, Your Highness. We tried to follow your orders but ... we failed you, Your Highness." The man bent his head, and a trickle of sweat slowly slid down to the tip of his nose where it halted for a brief moment before falling to the ground.

Tarragon closed his eyes from the short-lived distraction. For a moment there, it was as if time had been in slow motion. He shook his head and turned to frown at the engineer. "What's your name?"

"I apologize, Your Highness. Solas Epsin, First Engineer."

"What happened to the rest of your men?"

The muscle on Solas' cheek moved, as though he were gritting his teeth. "We took a hit the first round of attack three days ago, Your Highness. The four of us"—he pointed his thumb over his shoulder toward the three men behind him—"we were out repairing a generator so were spared. We're all that's left of the corps."

Tarragon pursed his lips and nodded. He remembered that day when they'd been caught unawares—just another indication that he knew absolutely nothing but theories and hypotheses when it came to warfare. Not for the first time, he sent up a curse to his father for his lack of military education. Taking a deep breath, he tilted his head toward the machine.

"What's wrong with the generators? Is it fuel? I thought we still had enough fuel to run them?"

"We do, but something's wrong." Solas turned around and pointed at a mangled piece of metal of what Tarragon assumed to be one of their generators. "We can't power them up. We thought at first, there was some sort of short in the circuits, but there's nothing we can find wrong with it. Electricity simply won't flow. It just died."

"Show me," Tarragon said.

Without a word, Solas led him the short distance to the machine.

"Is this it?" Tarragon examined the device. It looked rusty and distorted in a few places, but he knew from experience that it was the one piece of technology that their civilization had become highly dependent on in the past decade.

"Yes, Your Highness. I know it doesn't look like much, but this piece of technology is the main source of power that we need to light up the perimeter fence. Electrify it. So nothing goes through it without getting zapped."

"Help me down, I need to see what's inside it," Tarragon said.

Again, the engineer did not question his orders, but Tarragon didn't miss the way the engineer threw a meaningful look at the soldier before moving to assist him. Tarragon ignored them. Without another word, Solas stepped forward and offered a hand to help Tarragon lower himself carefully to the ground. As he crouched, the pain in his leg drew an involuntary hiss from him. Momentarily distracted from his task, he closed his eyes and gripped tightly on the soldier's forearm, drawing in breaths to steady himself. When the throbbing subsided to barely tolerable, he opened his eyes once more and slowly lowered himself.

Once he was on the ground, he peered under the base of the machine and touched the metal with his fingertips, feeling the cool, smooth surface. As a young boy, he'd always felt a pull toward technology, especially things that ran on electricity. Today, hurt and weak from his injuries, he felt the pull gaining strength, and he couldn't ignore it. He hadn't the vigor to fight it like his father had insisted he did, so he allowed the energy to come into him and communicate with him.

He'd never let anyone know his secret, and he guessed he never would tell, but he wished he could tell them now. Just by being this close to the innocuous looking piece of technology, he was already beginning to feel energized. Once he detected the tiny electrical vibrations, he closed his eyes and concentrated. He allowed his mind to empty of all thoughts, reached out with his senses, and listened to the machine. That was another secret he'd kept from everyone — that somehow, he could visualize what was going on wrong or right in a piece of machinery. He felt the pulse of energy and moved his torso — making it so no one behind him would see what he knew would be suspected as magic. Just as he did, he felt a flash of energy enter through his skin. The weak tingling sensation immediately renewed his flagging strength — it was as though the electricity were healing him from inside out. He opened his eyes, wanting to see what, up to now, he could never verbalize.

Tarragon deepened his focus until he saw the thin tendrils of blue flame appear. It tickled his skin, making Tarragon smile in relief. When he thanked it, the blue tendrils jerked as though the flame had heard him, and then it began to pulse stronger. Seemingly emboldened by his acknowledgment, the tendrils branched out further and faster, spreading across his hand in a heartbeat. Tarragon continued to encourage the force, sending more positive thoughts to help strengthen it when it paused. He felt it gain in confidence in response. Soon Tarragon's entire hand was covered with the blue light, the feeling of delight and acceptance flooding his mind.

"Later. Now, light it up," he breathed out softly.

The crack of the generator coming to life resounded across the camp. The posts along the perimeter walls lit up in an explosion of blue light that began from the post nearest Tarragon. One by one, the posts around the camp lit up, the blue glow fading into a blinding white light.

Breathing out his thanks to the machine, Tarragon patted the delightfully humming metal before shifting himself so he could rise. In doing so, he looked up and into the face of the soldier. Their gazes locked and held in what felt like eons. There was no sign in the violet gaze that it had witnessed Tarragon's taboo deeds. Tarragon shifted his focus and looked at the engineers who were standing in silence, gaping at him.

"Can anyone help me up?"

The soldier looked startled at the sound of his voice but didn't hesitate to rush in to help Tarragon up to his feet. Tarragon brushed his hands down his clothes, and as he leaned over to clear his legs of the dust that might infect his wound, he noticed that the puncture wound there had closed. The redness that had surrounded the wound had also faded to a healthier pink. For a moment, Tarragon was too startled to speak, but he blinked his surprise away when he heard the harsh, indrawn breath from the soldier.

"Your leg. It's healed," the man muttered, motioning to Tarragon's leg.

Tarragon opened his mouth to say something when an explosion from the front of their camp ripped the words from him. He crouched low, throwing his hands over his head. When the dust settled, he looked up, and he saw men hurled in all directions. He recognized two of the engineers who'd only just recently helped him. Another was crawling toward them. It was Solas.

"Your Highness, come with me."

Tarragon tore his gaze away to look at the soldier who had shouted at him. The soldier reached out and grabbed onto Tarragon's arm before pulling him away. Tarragon didn't question the man, simply crouched low on the ground and ran as fast as he could. Their camp had been breached, but the generator that he'd cajoled back to life continued to hum and power the perimeter fence. It flashed and threw out sparks as bodies hit the wires. Tarragon reached out to the generator and instructed it to send more power to the fence. That it needed to hold on, not to falter, and it needed to block the enemy soldiers from breaking through. In response, the generator hummed louder. Tarragon thanked it once more, but he knew the generator wouldn't be able to hold on for long. It just needed to do its work until Tarragon could get his men to safety. All around him, soldiers rushed, screaming as they sprang to arms and engaged those who had assaulted them.

"Take cover!" Tarragon called out to his men even as he dove under a cart. He crawled under the confined space, cursing under his breath when bodies fell around him, thrashing in death throes. Some were still alive but were groaning in mortal pain. A hard thud from above him made him flinch. He looked up and saw a twitching leg hanging from the edge of the cart. Tears of frustration flooded his eyes. His men were being killed all around him, and here he was, cowering under a cart like a coward. He had to do something. But just then, something inside his mind snapped, and he suddenly felt emptied of his soul. Inside his chest, a ripping agony, not quite unlike what he'd felt from his leg earlier, threatened to make him gag. He opened his mouth to scream even as everywhere around him screams of pain and loss came from his men.

The soldier who had helped him earlier lay as if in a daze. He'd stood before the cart to defend Tarragon's cover but now lay on the ground, tears sliding down the side of his temples, his mouth open in abject misery and terror.

Tarragon closed his eyes as a sob escaped his own lips. Something was wrong. Something had gone terribly wrong.

He knew what had happened. Somehow, his father, who had left him to take command of this encampment only two weeks before, was dead. Tarragon knew that with certainty. He had felt his father's hold on his mind brutally cut off. The ripping of his soul as it left his body was nothing like how he'd felt when his brothers had been ambushed and killed years before. But unlike his brothers, Tarragon's father had no one to hand over his collective memories to.

Their family had always been unique. The Dacron clan rulers had been born with a gift only the mages of the mountains were thought to possess. But unlike the mages, the Dacron clan had kept it secret, so had been spared the bigotry and retained its status and rank among the royal families of Oryon.

Mages were abhorred. Not because of their power, but because people feared them. The Zaruthrans and the Capricis had attacked Tarragon's family because their suspicions had spurred on that hatred and fear. Dacron kings always had heirs, sons and daughters, who'd stood waiting until such time as they'd received the collective gift of their fathers. With the combined knowledge, each ascending king or queen, no matter their age, had the capacity to rule. Although Tarragon and his father had been spared the massacre, when his brothers were lost, it had been his father who had borne the brunt of his sons' transfers. Tarragon had been too sick to accompany his father and brothers to the capital city. When the attack came, his brothers had been out hunting with other delegates, while their father had been in a conclave nearby with the other kings of Oryon. And now, Tarragon knew he was the last of his line. He knew his lease on life was running out. He was being hunted—but by the Goddess, he was no prey.

Spurred on by the knowledge, he knew if he didn't do anything, not only would he die, but so would his entire clan. The vassals and soldiers whose families had served the Dacron kings for hundreds of generations stood on the brink of annihilation. With a will he couldn't fathom the source of, he crawled on his belly toward the edge of the cart. Once there, he heaved himself from under it and reached out for the soldier still lying prostrate in front of the cart. He cursed under his breath. He had no idea what the man's name was—time to rectify the situation.

"Soldier," he snapped out. "Name and rank."

The man blinked blindly and shook his head before turning to face him. His eyes were wide in surprise, the pain of loss deepening the violet in them. Tarragon watched him swallow as though to clear his throat.

"Brenn. Lieutenant Brenn, Your Highness." Brenn's voice sounded gritty.

"Guardian Brenn, on your feet and do your duty," Tarragon commanded.

At first, Brenn blinked at him in confusion, but then his expression changed to one of determination, and he slowly rose to his feet. Fist to chest, he saluted Tarragon and dipped his head in a bow of acknowledgment. As a Guardian, his rank had not only tripled in status but given him command over the soldiers left alive in the camp. Tarragon hoped he made the right decision. He knew nothing about this man. Yet something told him that Brenn was someone to be trusted.

"Your will, sire," Brenn said.

"Take as many able men you can find and burn everything to the ground. Let nothing stand in your way. We retreat. Take Solas with you. And see if the medic, Derek, is still alive. Last I saw him was yesterday tending to the wounded. Tell him we have need of his services."

No question met his orders. Brenn bowed stiffly and left, his movements hurried and determined. Tarragon hurried toward the generator he'd taken energy from. Through a spinning haze of fear and new-found resolve, he knew what he was about to do would break all of the rules his father and brothers had imposed on him since as far back as he could remember. No longer was he going to hide what he thought, that he was of mage descent. No longer was he going to hide his talents. His clan came first, and he would do anything to survive and save his family. The Zaruthrans and the Capricis would now have to deal with a talent they'd never before seen in a Dacron king.

Like a torch to fuel, the energy that Tarragon had long ago silenced rose inside him. His gaze locked on the humming generator. He didn't understand how it was he had an affinity to technology. No one had tutored him on what it was to be a mage. Scorned as they were, the mages hid and kept secret the knowledge of how to control their talent.

Tarragon studied the generator in quiet contemplation, unmindful of the explosions and cries of agony going about him. Compelled by the energy source, Tarragon laid his hands on the now heated machine and closed his eyes against the world.

Not quite like a gentle caress, a tingling, tickly feeling entered his skin. Tendrils of questioning energy requested access, and Tarragon gave it. He didn't understand the hows or whys of it, he just instinctively knew that this was going to be his life from now on.

Something moved by his side, and the energy reacted to the threat. Without opening his eyes, Tarragon dispatched

what he somehow knew to be an enemy soldier in a reflex-
ive slash of his free hand. The energy talked to him, told him
things with no words or feelings, only images. The energy
screamed. A slash of burning pain dropped across his
shoulder, and Tarragon cried out, his right arm losing feeling. But his left hand remained on the generator's surface,
and that touch opened a bright world of blue and white rage
in his mind. On a thought and a mutter of a word, Tarragon's deadened arm functioned once more. He opened his
eyes and saw an enemy soldier standing at an arm's length
from him. He watched as the man raised his sword over his
head in a two-handed hold. With a flick of his finger, blue
energy rushed the length of Tarragon's arm, ran down to the
tips of his fingers, and leapt through the space between him
and death. The enemy stood frozen, his mouth open in a
wordless scream. Seconds passed as though hours had, and
then the enemy began to crumble, falling to the ground in a
pile of dark ash.

Tarragon's lips curled into a grim smile—his powers finally acknowledged and given voice. Turning to face the
battle that raged across the camp, Tarragon watched men
struggle in a dance to death, their swords and knives glinted
red in the glow of white light from the perimeter walls. In
the distance, he saw a lone figure. It was Brenn, and he stood
as though frozen. Their gazes met, and Tarragon knew that
Brenn had again witnessed what Tarragon had done. Tarragon tilted his head to the side, issuing a challenge to the one
who was first to observe the rise of a mage king. Expecting
to see condemnation, Tarragon stood ready to defend
himself.

But Brenn didn't betray him. His face set in an expression
Tarragon could not interpret, Brenn raised the flat of his
sword to his lips, kissed the blade, then pointed it toward
Tarragon. It was a salute, a clear confirmation that Tarra-

gon's action had been seen and acknowledged. But Brenn continued to surprise Tarragon. He lowered his sword and turned around to give further instructions to the waiting soldiers.

Standing in the middle of a scene straight from hell, Tarragon breathed a sigh of relief. Explanations would have to be given, but that could wait. Now he had an enemy to defeat. First, it would be the Zaruthran soldiers. Second would be the Capricis. One by one, Tarragon felled the enemy with the blue flame of his talent. He no longer cared about what his men witnessed. Foremost in his mind was his men's safety. When the dust finally settled on what Tarragon instinctively knew would be a victory never before seen on Oryon, he would deal with the mages. It was time for them to choose sides and be acknowledged.

Now, if only he could find where it was they were hiding.

CHAPTER TWO

Three months after their narrow escape, Tarragon found himself kneeling in the middle of the grand foyer of Dacron Palace. His hand trembled as skin touched stone, but it was not from the dropping temperature. Deep inside, his mind rebelled, screamed its denial, but his resolve to remain calm overrode whatever rising panic he felt. From outside, he heard the distinctive sound of a death gong. The sound reverberated between his ears, the solitary note echoed back and forth, diminishing all other thought. It was a ghost of a sound, and yet it held within it — everything.

A shiver coursed through his body, but again, it was not from a chill, but from the weight of responsibility. He glanced to his left where Brenn stood in the shadows by the walls. The man had not left his side ever since they'd escaped the encampment three months before. Together, they had led their men in retreat. If his father were still alive, he knew that he would have been whipped for acting a coward. But Tarragon was no coward. If he'd not left that area, he and his men would have been slaughtered by enemy reinforcements that would have eventually joined their comrades. No. It had not been a cowardly move to relocate his men to safety. He needed to heal. No, they all needed to heal. None of them would have recovered from their wounds if they had stayed in the mountains. So he'd thought to bring them all home, to the land of his forebears.

For three months, he and Brenn had rallied what was left of his army back to safety, encouraging them to move on, to

17

deny their pain, to hope for their homes. But when they had arrived, they had faced even more tragedy. Outside, the gong chimed again, but still, Tarragon paid it no heed. Today, Tarragon found himself the last of the royal line of Dacron. He'd expected to see at least one or two of his sisters-in-law, foul-tempered though they might have been, but they had been the widows of his brothers and mothers to his nephews and nieces. They were the only family left.

Or so he'd hoped.

None of them had been there to meet him. In fact, no one had been left alive to meet his sorry company.

Whoever had broken through the gates into the palace compound had killed what had been the last of his family. The action had been wrought with cruel intent and vengeance. Save for the plants, not even the animals had been spared. Everyone had been killed. Murdered. It was as if his family's enemies had wanted the whole of Dacron erased from the face of Oryon.

Once again, the gong sounded, deep and rich. Mournful. Angry. Tarragon closed his eyes a moment and prayed to the Goddess. He begged for guidance and comfort. Why was he plagued with doubts? He knew what he was expected to do by everyone. If his enemies thought him alive, they expected him to surrender. If his enemies knew he was still alive, they would hunt him to the ground and kill him. Surrender or death — there was really no choice.

Tarragon knew for a certainty his enemies thought him dead, and if so, they had done what anyone would have done to the remaining live members of his family. Kill them all so they could take over without anyone opposing or challenging them. But they were mistaken in their assumption. When another gong was struck, Tarragon could not help but flinch at the sound. Every sound meant a tribute to those who had perished under enemy hands, and as of that second, Tarragon had already lost count. Tears falling, his heart breaking, Tarragon slowly rose from the floor.

He looked up at Dacron Palace. Whoever the butchers were, they had spared the structure, most likely thinking they would move in and take over it completely after the proper period of time was passed. By tradition, the homes of the defeated would be left alone for at least three years before a priest came by to banish any remnants of those who had dwelled in them. That meant that Tarragon had enough time to have it cleared without the distraction of his enemies knocking on his door. That was three years he had every intention of using to gather his forces in secret. His only question was whether those he sought to bring into his company were even willing to join him. He turned toward Brenn.

"Have those who are able clear out the dead and rubble. As for the rest, let them find rooms for everyone. No one is to sleep outside the palace. Leave all the dwellings outside as they are for now, and instead, have some men search for food and supplies. Whoever did this most assuredly cleaned us out, but it would help to keep their minds busy."

"What about weapons, sire?"

Tarragon's heart wrenched at the title. Ever since his father's death, he had denied the fact that he was technically the king, but Brenn had continued to use it since then. He had not sought to correct his man, but he had also not been affected by its use. Until today. Today, it was as if the scales had been lifted from over his eyes. Today, there was a reality he could no longer ignore.

"I don't think there are any left in storage. Tell the men they have a week to finish their tasks. Also, don't send out word that we are still alive, or that there is still a living, breathing Dacron left. When you're done giving your orders, come to me. We have much to discuss."

Brenn didn't reply. He merely bowed his head, turned

around, and walked through the doorway. He descended the stairs to the courtyard below to where Tarragon knew the surviving company of servants and guards stood waiting under the dimming sky. Several wore bandages, and most had torn and bloody clothes. Tarragon looked up as another gong was struck. His gaze went to a lone figure in the distance. One of the soldiers had taken it upon himself to give honor to the dead. Tarragon didn't need to see that far to recognize Solas Espin's bulky figure. It was not an easy task, for the gong was placed atop a parapet. It could only be reached if someone were strong enough to climb the more than four hundred steps. None of the servants and soldiers openly displayed their grief other than placing their fists over their hearts and bowing their heads when Tarragon had come into view.

Tarragon had followed Brenn a few steps behind. He stood at the doorway and watched as Brenn walked over to a battle-scarred soldier, erect and proud despite his lifetime of loyal service. Tarragon recognized Derek, a medic who had steadfastly made sure they survived the mountain pass they'd had to cross. It was he who made sure that their wounds had been cleaned and bandaged and their dead buried. Miraculously, he still stood on his two legs. From the deep lines on his face, he looked exhausted as well. Just like they all were.

Together, Brenn and Derek walked through the rest of the company. He remembered how brave they had all looked in their armor and uniforms years before, especially his father, with the bright green plume of his helmet. They had been so full of confidence, their chests expanded, their shoulders back, their grins broad. Oh, those were the days of the Dacron pride. Now? Tarragon's heart clenched at the sight. Before him were a raggedly bunch who wore tattered clothes. Most had lost their weapons, but thankfully, not their *septurecces*. The resilient and sturdy animals had carried their sorry bodies through the mountain pass with little to no discomfort. At least with their beasts, they still held a semblance of what had been a formidable army.

Tarragon watched Brenn do his bidding, and not for the first time, was thankful that he had someone he could trust and who could act as his right hand. Without another thought, he turned around and reentered the dim corridors of the palace in search of his rooms. His mind continued to rebel, screamed louder its denial, but he stamped his rising panic. There was time enough to grieve and plan.

Today was his eighteenth birthday. Today, there would be no cause for celebration. Today, he would bury his family.

CHAPTER THREE

Tarragon had never felt this exhausted before, not even during their trek through the mountains to reach Dacron Palace. But now, a day after they'd arrived at the palace, he settled himself in the bath he'd drawn in his bathing room and felt every muscle fiber scream in agony. He closed his eyes and began to think. He knew he must rise from his grief and panic so he could plan the next course of action. His father's enemies had been many. It was not surprising that the man had been a bully. But the murder of his brothers, their wives, and their children, that was inexcusable. They had been innocent. In truth, they had also borne the brunt of their king's cruelty. No. There was another reason why his enemies sought the obliteration of the Dacron. The enmity had only started during his father's time—surely there was another reason why they sought the family's destruction. Their secret had been theirs to keep. Who had betrayed them? He thought about what was left of his men—the Dacron army was obviously greatly weakened. He hoped that some of the men his father had brought with him had survived their defeat. It was a shallow hope, seeing what had been done here, but he needed that hope.

For a long while, Tarragon soaked in the tub. His clan's position was bitterly clear. All that remained between his clan and those of the Capricis and Zaruthrans was him—a young, eighteen-year-old who had received no education or training on how to rule or command. The realization left a bad taste in his mouth. How was he to survive long enough to regain what had been lost? So far, he had no resources, only plots and plans that most likely would not work. He must find a way to increase his armies so he could fight and defeat his enemies.

Tarragon blinked and forced himself to get out of the rapidly cooling water. He had dreamed his plans, analyzed the twists and turns for each and come up with an almost impossible solution. There was only one way he could defeat his enemies. He had already embraced his magic, but there was only so much he could do with it without having to learn everything about it. What good was his talent and position if he didn't know how to wield it properly and safely? He knew only of one group of people who could help him. He needed to find the mages and embrace them into his clan. The problem was, where to start, where to find them, and whether he even survive his encounter with them. The mages were scorned for a reason. They were powerful, they had magic, they were long-lived, and they were highly secretive, to the point of murder.

Tarragon left his rooms, dressed in fresh clothes he'd found in one of his brothers' closet. He'd been surprised how small his old clothes were when he'd attempted to put them on. As he stepped into the borrowed pants, he couldn't comprehend why they were still there, while the rest of his family was not. It seemed ironic somehow that their clothes had survived. Most likely, the other rooms would hold the rest of his brothers' things. He'd thought there would have at least been some looting, but curiously, there had been none. As he walked through the corridors, he kept his focus forward, toward the turn where the stairs leading to the lower floors would be. Just like his unraided closet, the familiar statues and paintings that lined the walls were still there. True, they were dusty, but otherwise untouched. Tarragon gritted his teeth. His enemies had most likely ordered whoever had come here not to touch what they had seen as their future possessions. Well, they were never going to lay their hands on them. These were Dacron possessions, and by the Goddess, they were going to remain Dacron possessions.

He paused at the landing, observing the men moving and clearing the rubble on the first floor. There had been fighting here, it was clear as day to Tarragon, but at least, there were no blood stains to ruin the floors, walls or carpets. He still had to find out where his sisters-in-law and nephews and nieces' bodies were. Somehow, he had a feeling that they had been corralled with the servants who had remained and killed with them. Where, he didn't want to know, but he needed to know.

Tarragon looked about him, ignoring the noise of the servants working to make the palace habitable. The impact of the change struck Tarragon hard. No longer could he see innumerable servants silently moving about as they did their daily chores. There were no longer countless soldiers dressed in perfectly fitted uniforms to line the halls and guard their posts. What hit him hardest was the lack of children's laughter as they ran every which way they could, unmindful of their mothers' ire or their watchers' cautions. Absently, he wondered who he could appoint as overseer of the household and properties. If he still had properties to oversee, that was. He searched for Brenn's lithe form, feeling the need to discuss the matter with him. A soldier stepped up to him, obscuring his view of the courtyard. The man bowed his head as he waited for Tarragon to acknowledge him.

"What is it?" Tarragon asked, clenching his hands on the hilt of his sword.

"Sire, Guardian Brenn asked me to tell you that he has found your family," the man said formally.

Tarragon's heart stuttered in his chest, but he fought hard to keep his face impassive.

"Where?"

"We found them in the temple. I can lead you there, sire."

"Are the others there as well?"

"Yes, sire. Everyone is there."

"Take me. Now," Tarragon snapped. Then, remembering that most likely this man had lost his family in the massacre as well, he took a deep breath and placed a comforting hand on his shoulder. "Please."

The man lowered his head and gave a brief nod before turning on his heel to lead the way. Tarragon kept his focus forward as he moved outside the palace doors toward the gardens to the side of it where the private royal temple to the Goddess stood. The soldier kept his pace steady, and from the way his shoulders were set, it was apparent to Tarragon that the man was having difficulty controlling his emotions. On instinct, Tarragon reached out to the man's mind. At his touch, the shoulders immediately relaxed. Tarragon held on to his mind and soothed it, thankful that he could help. Other soldiers moved closer to them and once more, Tarragon reached out with his mind and touched theirs. Immediately, the men moved to flank his sides, their hands reaching out to touch his clothes. Tarragon didn't mind their touches. He'd seen this before, with his father and brothers.

As his soldiers ushered him toward the temple, Tarragon wished for somewhere quiet and dark to hide in to confront his own sorrow. But the instant he stepped up on the stairs leading inside, Brenn stepped up in front of him, barring his way. He bowed his head briefly before stepping up toward Tarragon.

Tarragon automatically returned his Guardian's salute and saw that Brenn had taken advantage of a bath as well.

The uniform he was wearing looked bright compared to what the other soldiers were wearing. Tarragon didn't know where he got it, but it fit him well, although when he glanced down, the sleeves were a little short on the cuff.

"Sire, you don't want to go in there."

The world tilted at an angle, but Tarragon fought on. "How many?"

"Everyone who had been left here, sire."

"How many?"

When Brenn didn't answer, Tarragon stepped forward until he was nose to nose with Brenn.

"How did they die?"

Brenn's gaze met his. They held on until, as though a dam had burst, his eyes filled with tears.

"Burned, sire. They were burned."

"My sisters-in-law? My nephews? My nieces?"

"Yes, sire. All of them. Also the priests, servants, even their pets are in there, sire. Please. Don't go in there. Please."

Tarragon nodded, letting his eyes close for a long second. Softly, he said, "Very well." He wished he could hide, anywhere, so he could scream, somewhere impossible to find and be in without showing his weakness. He could not afford to show weakness.

Brenn's voice cut through the air as he shouted out his commands. Tarragon turned on his heel and walked the way he came. His mind was a confused jumble of thoughts of his brothers' wives and children. *Sixteen innocent souls.*

He finally reached the gardens at the back of the palace, his knees nearly buckling from the force of his trembling. His hand found purchase on a bark of a tree, and he leaned on it, grateful that something could hold him up. He would remember the way there, even if he were dying, he would know the way. His feet knew the path well, down to the crooked stone path in front of the iron gates. The hedge was just as thick and manicured as he'd remembered it, its snow-white petalled flowers as fragrant as ever. It shielded the gardens from outside.

Straightening, Tarragon looked toward the well and walked the short distance to it. He leaned over its depths. It was clean of any debris or bodies, and the pail still hung there. Mindlessly, he loosened the ropes that held the pail and lowered it. When he felt the weight of the pail pull on the ropes, he raised it again in sure, even motions. When the pail emerged from the depths, he saw that the water was clean and fresh. Another wonder to add to the already confusing situation. Why had they left the well untouched? But no matter. It didn't matter. With one hand, Tarragon gripped the handle and took it and brought it toward the bed of flowers his mother had planted all those years ago. Before his birth. Before she died giving birth to him. Before the betrayals that had killed his brothers. Before his father lost control and taken out his frustrations on him.

Tarragon lost track of time, focused on his task of watering his mother's garden, knowing that Brenn would take care of things, that he would make sure everyone he loved was buried and given the Goddess' blessing. He hoped Brenn would find a priest or priestess, but he doubted it. The blessings could still be given by lay people, like Brenn. He didn't feel guilty for not being in attendance. He wanted to remember them as they had been, happy and full of laughter. Not burned to a crisp.

He took his time, losing himself in memories amidst the sweet-blossomed fruit trees. There was a pond, its surface rippling faintly, reflecting the blue of the sky. Overhead, a curtain of drooping branches hung heavy with ripening fruit. For a moment he stopped to examine them, calculating the time of harvest. It wouldn't be long, maybe a week or so, and they would be ripe enough. Before the weather turned.

It would be soon. They would do well in the storage houses. Hopefully, those structures would be as untouched as the others were. They were cool inside and would preserve the fruits for months.

As he watered the plants, memories returned of the older brothers he had loved and looked up to like breath in his lungs. Magnus with the twinkling green eyes and ready smile for his youngest brother. Konrad who had wielded his battle ax stronger and surer than the more experienced warriors of the king's house. Franco, the brother closest to Tarragon's age, the one who rode his horse the fastest and drew his arrow the surest, a feat that had remained unmatched even after his death. His brothers had always had time for Tarragon, and they always made sure he was kept from their father's wrath. They had taken it upon themselves to start his training. He remembered how Konrad would always tell a stupid joke, usually involving risqué topics that would bring the young Tarragon to laugh and wish he were older so he could join in his brothers' activities. He could even remember how his father, the king, a man who rarely smiled, would laugh out loud at Konrad's tales. Tarragon had never loved his father, but as king, he had respected him. His brothers, though, he had loved them. Grief swooped over him, like an eagle to its prey, and it engulfed his senses.

He didn't notice the sun sinking or when the lights overhead were switched on. He didn't raise his head when the funeral chant rose from the direction of the temple. He didn't say a word when Brenn stepped in to join him in his efforts. He didn't mind when more soldiers joined him. They had taken up pails of their own and helped in watering the entire garden with him. When he felt a mind rip apart in pain and anguish, he reached out toward it. He did so without thinking and held it gently in his. He held it until he soothed the rip to seal and come together once more. When another mind screamed in distress, he reached toward it, seized it, and comforted it. More tortured minds came, and Tarragon met them head-on, took hold of each of them in his mind without thought or consideration of his own pain.

When the dawn light finally came, Tarragon found himself in his bed. He didn't know how he'd come to his rooms, but he remembered leaning onto the one who had taken him there. There he'd lain, wrapped in the strong arms, looking out to the morning sky that was filled with birds flying in the wind, listening to their cries, weeping uncontrollably. He screamed in terror at the future he knew was to come, and he leaned into the arms that had tightened around him. But even in the pain of his epiphany, he never let go of his clan's mind and psyche. Instead, he gave them courage. He gave them hope. He poured out his strength into them. Showed them the way. Showed them the plan.

Finally, when the storm passed, Tarragon, the last prince of the Dacron clan, acknowledged the inevitable. He had come face to face with his fate.

He was king.

CHAPTER FOUR

Tarragon slowly worked his hand under the blanket until he found Brenn's stiffening cock. He'd opened his eyes to a gray morning. The mist that formed in front of him as he yawned clued him on the temperature outside. It was finally winter, and the mountain pass they'd meticulously blocked with as many boulders and traps as they could fashion had taken him and his men weeks to finish. Yesterday had been that day, and he had sought the comfort of his bed as soon as he reached the palace. He'd waved off the servant who'd been assigned to him, telling him not to bother waking him for dinner. When he'd finally woken minutes earlier, he felt the familiar warm body that lay next to his.

After that first night, Brenn had slept with him, sometimes on the floor, but most times, he crawled in beside Tarragon and kept him close in his arms. Tarragon wished he didn't suffer the nightmares that plagued his sleep, but no matter how rested or tired he was, the horrible images kept creeping in to terrorize him. Brenn helped keep them at bay, and he'd grown accustomed to waking up next to his Guardian. Only Tarragon was getting too attached to that hard, muscled body, and this morning he could no longer resist. So, the morning light found Tarragon gazing hungrily at his Guardian's face, longing to touch the lashes that curled from his lids, then looking down to Brenn's mouth, where his gaze lingered, wanting . . . no . . . needing to taste the forbidden. Brenn shifted in his sleep, and Tarragon's gaze drifted even lower, down to where the top of the sheet had lowered, and he felt his fingers twitch. The need to trail the dark sprinkling of hair there made Tarragon's mouth water. He wondered what his Guardian would do should he wake to his king's mouth licking his shaft. But first, he needed to touch.

Tarragon knew Brenn was coming to awareness when he folded his fingers over the hot, thickening shaft he now held. Brenn's breathing labored, as though he were startling to awareness. Tarragon saw Brenn's stomach tense, and he tightened his hold, working it up and down, making the cock stiffen even more.

"Sire?" Brenn breathed deeply, like he'd run a race.

Tarragon looked up. "Call me by my name, Brenn."

Brenn's breath hitched and his legs shifted, but he didn't move away. Just to make sure, Tarragon tightened his hold even more, making the drags slower, and tighter, heating the sensitive skin there.

"I said, call me by my name, Brenn," Tarragon said when Brenn didn't speak.

"Tarragon, what are you doing?" Brenn's voice sounded low and gravelly, but Tarragon noticed that he didn't move away or complain about what he was doing.

The need to taste rose high and Tarragon didn't wait for Brenn to push him away. Quickly, he moved until he was at the level of Brenn's crotch. Without wasting time, he dropped his head, opened his mouth and took Brenn's cock into his mouth in one move. The groan coming from above rumbled its way down, and Tarragon used his tongue to stroke on the thick vein and then around the bulbous head. He could taste the bitterness of precum, and for a moment, he paused to savor it.

Tarragon was dimly aware of Brenn shifting under him, and then he felt a hand over his head. At first, it simply lay there, but then the fingers entwined into his hair in a tight hold. The next few minutes were lost in the heat, smell, and taste of Brenn, and Tarragon loved every second of it. No way was he ever going to forget Brenn's taste. Until he died, he would always remember the uniqueness of it, and he knew, he just knew, he would never find another like it. He lost himself in making sure that Brenn would find that pleasure Tarragon was giving him.

When Brenn finally came in Tarragon's mouth, his cry of ecstasy made him proud. He'd done that to the man. Him. Brenn's hips arched off the bed, thrusting his cock deeper into Tarragon's mouth, the bulbous head touching the back of his throat. Finally, when Brenn was spent, Tarragon couldn't help the smile that spread over his lips, but he kept his face down as he used his tongue to lick Brenn's arousal down until it fell limply in his hands. When Brenn's breathing calmed, he reached out and cupped Tarragon's face. Brenn drew him up until Tarragon lay against Brenn's chest, his arms holding him firmly close. He could hear Brenn's heart beating erratically and somehow, that made Tarragon feel even prouder than he already was.

"Why did you do that?" Brenn asked quietly. His violet eyes were wide, as though he still hadn't gotten over the surprise that had woken him.

"You're very hard to resist," Tarragon said, his lips pulling into a smile. "If I know myself well, I can never find satisfaction until I've had a taste of temptation." He leaned over and kissed Brenn on his lips, knowing that the man would taste himself on Tarragon's lips. When they parted, Brenn's look was a combination of shock and satisfaction. It was a curious mix—it was as if he didn't know what to think of Tarragon's actions.

Tarragon moved off Brenn and stood by the bed, looking down at him. He held out his hand, which Brenn took silently, though his eyes still regarded him intently. Tarragon led him to the bathing chamber and stepped under the warm spray. He closed his eyes and relaxed under the water, waiting for Brenn's next move. He smiled to himself when he felt rather than heard Brenn step in behind him. When Brenn closed his arms around his chest, Tarragon turned until they came face to face.

"What are you thinking about?" Tarragon held his hand under a spout that came out from one side of the wall and watched as a clear, blue gel dribbled into his palm. He rubbed his palms together, allowing the suds to develop before rubbing them over Brenn's chest.

"I'm thinking that you are a naughty brat and that I've underestimated you."

Tarragon raised a brow. "Did you want me to stop?"

Brenn let out a huff and put his hand under the spout. As he washed Tarragon's back, he bit on his lower lip, making Tarragon think that Brenn was having a difficult time processing what had just happened between them. When he was done with Tarragon's back, Brenn reached out for more soap and began to wash Tarragon's thighs. His hands lingered over Tarragon's cock. He licked his lips but didn't do anything other than soap the rest of Tarragon's body.

"Do you want to taste me?"

Brenn's head shot up, and their gazes met. Brenn's eyes were filled with doubt, but there was also an unmistakable need. Tarragon thrust out his hips, his cock lengthening, hardening under the water, inviting Brenn to look down where his gaze locked. The heat rose in Tarragon once more, and his cock straightened directly in front of Brenn's mouth. Thankfully, the temptation proved too much, for Brenn took Tarragon's hips in his hands and swallowed the waiting cock into his mouth.

Tarragon moved until his back hit the wall. He waved his hand in front of the control panel, and the water warmed up some more. Up and down Brenn moved over his cock, and there was nothing for Tarragon to do but roll his head against the wall and wait for that inevitable.

Brenn's movements were steady, but the force of his suction made Tarragon's breathing labored. The sureness of his movements, the timing of them, revealed Brenn was a skilled lover, and Tarragon couldn't help feeling jealous of those nameless, faceless past lovers. His eyes flew open when he felt a sharp nip at the tip of his cock, and he looked down to find that Brenn had taken it between his teeth. The look in his eyes, though, stilled Tarragon.

"Be careful, Tarr. Your thoughts betray you. I saw what you were thinking. Should I stop?"

"Don't you dare stop."

The corner of Brenn's mouth curled before he lowered his head once more to take Tarragon's cock into his mouth again. This second time around, Brenn didn't seem as controlled. This time, he sucked harder, he rolled Tarragon's balls in one hand while the other . . . .

Goddess, what Brenn was doing with that finger inside him nearly brought Tarragon to his knees. The dual sensations drowned all thought from his mind. It was all he could do to focus on the now.

Another finger? The stretch increased, and Tarragon held on to Brenn's shoulder. He raised a leg, hoping he wouldn't slip. Brenn continued his assault outside and inside of him, and Tarragon wanted to be filled.

"Brenn, I need you," he gasped out.

Without saying a word, Brenn released Tarragon's cock and stood. He turned Tarragon until his chest touched the wall where his back had been. Tarragon widened his stance, but he didn't have to wait long. Those fingers opened him, using something to slick him up, probably the soap, Tarragon didn't care. And then Brenn was inside him, long, and hard, and hot. In one quick move, he was up and inside of Tarragon and all Tarragon could do was hold on and hope he didn't slip on the wet tiles.

CHAPTER FIVE

A grim-faced Brenn handed him a hot drink after their shower and told him about his plans. "I'm taking some of the men with me. The ones who are able. The rest will stay here with you."

"Where are you going?"

"We're going to explore and search for survivors and make sure that passage through to here remains closed. It will probably take a few hours, but we'll back by tonight."

When Brenn stepped back to leave the room, Tarragon stopped him.

"Wait. That first time, why did you stay with me that night? I never got to ask." He could feel his face heat at the memory of being held in Brenn's arms that first time.

Brenn bowed his head. "You needed me here, sire. The others, they saw your pain. We all saw your pain. We all felt it. I just wanted to help."

"And after that?"

Brenn smiled. "I didn't want to leave."

Slowly, Tarragon got up, and once more, Brenn turned to go. Once more, Tarragon stopped him. "Brenn?"

Brenn turned back to face him. "Yes, sire?"

Tarragon smiled through the residual emotional pain. "Thank you, for everything."

"Sire," Brenn said, a small smile hovering over his lips.

This time, when he turned to go, Tarragon didn't stop him. He hurried to dress as warmly as he could.

Tarragon stopped breathless with one foot hovering over the first step down when he caught sight of Brenn and several men waiting in attention below the stairs.

"Was I that obvious?" Tarragon said when he finally joined Brenn.

Silently, Brenn checked Tarragon's attire, tugging on the wide leather belt that held the fur cape together and the weapons on his sides. When he was done with his inspection, he clacked his heels together and made a show of saluting Tarragon. As one, the soldiers in attendance did the same, the sounds of their heels sending echoes within the hall.

"All right, let's move out," Brenn said, his voice loud and stern.

On their way out the door, another soldier handed each of them a package wrapped in dry cloth and canisters of water. Tarragon checked his rations and looked at the soldier.

"That's your breakfast, sire. The rest of the rations have already been packed."

"Thank you," Tarragon said, then hurried out to join his men.

When he stepped out, he shivered almost immediately. The weather had finally turned, and the cold had descended upon them. His breath froze in a fog before him. He didn't have to ask Brenn why they had to move quickly. Soon the route they had to take would no longer be passable. Their enemies would have to wait several months for winter to lift, months that they could make full use to rally their forces or whoever there was left for them to rally. Tarragon had no doubt there were men out there, men and women who had survived the carnage.

The previous day, when he could no longer deny his sovereignty over his clan, he had felt those minds, and there were many out there. Most of them were confused and frightened, but more were angry and sought to avenge their loved ones. He would need to get to them and use their anger to fight their enemies.

The sharp brisk breeze added to the intensity of the bitter cold, and stinging rain made the six-legged beast snort and paw the hard ground. Tarragon sat astride his *septurecce* and surveyed the land beyond.

It was midday, and they had climbed into foothills, leaving behind the flatlands, far from the borders of the Dacron lands. When they'd left the compound, he had been accompanied by thirty of the more able men and had left the rest to straighten out the palace and the adjacent grounds. Brenn dispatched half of those men with instructions to make sure that the mountain path became impassable while the rest of them proceeded. No one complained that Brenn was keeping them at a man-killing pace. Tarragon didn't call Brenn out, either. He knew they needed to get through the high passes before nightfall.

Tarragon looked at the trees beyond and saw the thick boles and tangled brush. There were shadows everywhere, deep and dark, that could hide enemy and friend alike. Tarragon reached out with his mind and made a feel for mental energies. He opened his eyes to see Brenn watching him and gave a negative shake of his head. No. There were no hidden enemies about. The friendly ones were absent as well, so they continued their trek. Brenn's shoulders relaxed as he turned and waved their troop forward.

The sun climbed steadily overhead, but it didn't heat the rapidly dropping temperatures. No animals were scurrying about as they rambled across the distance. When they reached the crest of a rise, Brenn signaled a halt. At their riders' signal, the *septurecce* halted in their tracks, but the men maintained their position. Ahead, the road plunged a steep downward slope, winding into narrow turns and curves, then straightened to slice across and between the hills.

Two riders approached them swiftly from the side. Brenn, accompanied by two soldiers, rode off to meet them. Tarragon watched as the two riders stopped their *septurecce* before Brenn's and gave a salute. Their conversation didn't last long.

Brenn turned his *septurecce* around and approached Tarragon. He bowed his head briefly and pointed to the side.

"Sire, the scouts I sent ahead found signs of a recent encampment. The ashes were still warm. They also report to have found tracks going in the direction of the forest ahead."

Tarragon regarded the ravine, rubbing his palms together to warm them under the gloves he wore. He had worn heavy clothing for the trip, but the cold was turning bitter.

"Are you expecting any surprises?"

"I'm not sure," Brenn said, his gaze sweeping across their surroundings, as if by force of concentration he could see their enemies.

"I sense no one out there," Tarragon offered. "However, we must not be complacent. We must be prepared for anything that comes our way."

"I suggest we continue on," Brenn said.

"I agree. However, I fear the weather turning worse. We must find someplace safe to set up camp."

Brenn bowed his head briefly before turning back to the men to see to it that Tarragon's orders were carried out. One of the soldiers got down from his *septurecce* and hustled through the men with flasks of water. In silence, the man dispensed the drinks to the soldiers with a speed gained only through experience. Once all the men and beasts had been hydrated, Brenn signaled and gave the command to move out. Tarragon watched as the men followed his orders without question. It was as if Brenn had been born to command.

Tarragon strove hard to appear dignified and at ease, but the ache on his hands as he gripped on the reins hard grounded him. Deep inside, he prayed to the Goddess, asking for guidance.

When they reached the road beyond the crest, Tarragon lost himself to guiding his *septurecce* over the treacherous path. The road was covered with tiny loose stone. Thankfully, his beast didn't falter, although it did step over the path with care. Time and again, the gravel turned at a step and pebbles would bounce and rattle as they went over the edge. The treetops below them bore the brunt of the stones falling on their canopy. Tarragon forced himself not to look behind him and instead reached out to his men's minds. He breathed a sigh of relief when he found nothing but calm and determination.

Once they reached the bottom of the ravine, the dense trees spread on either side of them. The smell of the damp soil mixed with the aroma of the bark and leaves lingered heavily in the cold. It was a smell that was familiar to Tarragon, for he used to love the scent. But he didn't love it today. The air felt oppressive. As though his beast sensed his tension, his *septurecce* went rigid beneath him and made a nervous step to the side. Tarragon sat into the beast's back and made a comforting sound. His beast settled, but its trembling alerted Tarragon that something was not right.

Brenn stepped up to him and helped him get down from the beast. Once on the ground, Tarragon ran his hands over his beast's back. The beast's trembling settled under his touch.

"The beasts are restless, sire. Perhaps we should continue on and find a place to set up camp."

Tarragon nodded and ran his hand one last time over the *septurecce's* hindquarters. The beast no longer trembled, but its ears continued to flick back and forth, and its eyes darted nervously from Tarragon and into the forest.

"I don't think we should go there," Tarragon said in a calm, conversational tone.

"I agree, but we can't stay out here in the open," Brenn said, his own gaze directed into the dark of the forest.

"I don't think there's any use hiding, Brenn. Anyone going down that path could be seen from down here. I think it's not necessary to hide . . . we've already been seen."

"You're right, but I still don't like it," Brenn said.

"Then let's set up camp here, out in the open. I checked for hostile thoughts . . . I didn't find any out there. I have touched a curious mind or two, though, so they *are* out there." Tarragon turned his gaze back into the forest. "We just need to show them that we're not their enemy."

Chapter Six

"Your tent is ready. The men will see that you're safe." Brenn pointed to the center of the camp before taking the reins from Tarragon's hand.

Tarragon surrendered the reins, and with a last soothing caress down the *septurecce's* back, he turned to leave. But he didn't go toward where his tent stood. Instead, he decided to examine their immediate surroundings.

The frozen twigs and leaves crunched beneath his feet. He jabbed the earth with a booted foot, wondering what secrets it kept. He knew there were people out there, but as he hadn't received his father's gift of memories, he had to find their minds one at a time.

"Sire?"

Roused from his thoughts, he looked up to see Brenn had joined him. He had a jug of water in his hand. Taking it with a whispered thanks, he sipped the cold water. A dribble escaped and fell to his neck, making him shiver. Around them, the wood was still, and it was as if every living thing was already in hibernation or was too scared of their alien presence. He shivered once more, suddenly chilled as a brisk breeze flew from somewhere behind him. He looked over his shoulder and into the forest.

"What is it, sire?" Brenn asked, his voice low and full of tension.

Wordlessly, Tarragon gave the jug back to Brenn who set it on a nearby flat-topped stone. When he stood, the leather of his armor squeaked.

"I can sense them in there. They are just observing us from a distance . . . I can't tell how far. But they're there."

"Are they going to attack?"

Brenn's question surprised Tarragon, but he shrugged it off and closed his eyes. Gently, he reached out with his mind, searching through space, until, at last, he heard a thought.

I have to be strong. I have to fight. Goddess, when will they go away? When will they leave us alone?

Tarragon opened his eyes and looked back at Brenn, who stood with his hand holding the hilt of his sword.

"I think it unlikely. The thought I heard was more scared and desperate than resolved with the intent to attack us."

"Scared and desperate men act before they think," Brenn said, not taking his gaze off from the forest. Suddenly, a flock of birds flew up to the sky, their loud cries and flap of wings breaking the deep silence.

A shout erupted from the edge of the clearing and Tarragon felt Brenn's strong hands thrust him back. His ankle twisted and he fought for balance until he jerked himself upright.

Just then, Brenn whipped out his sword. It was different from the one he usually carried. This one was about six feet in length and a hand span wide. Intricate in design, it had a wide base that gradually narrowed to the broad tip. Its black handle cradled the black blade.

Tarragon narrowed his brows. He had never seen a sword that intricately designed. It looked more like a master's sword than a common soldier's. From where he stood, it was hard to discern the actual design, but it seemed as if the carvings on the flat side of the blade were bathed with a dim, blue glow. When Tarragon blinked, the glow had disappeared, and the sword looked just like any other metal weapon, only certainly more valuable than it pretended to look.

Pretended. Now, why would he think that?

Tarragon narrowed his focus and tentatively reached out with his mind, not expecting to get a response from the inanimate object. To his shock, the sword greeted him as if it knew him. There were no words, and he swore that while it greeted him, it also felt like it had reached inside his mind and tapped into his thoughts. Even more surprising, Tarragon didn't feel threatened. He could sense nothing but curiosity. All thoughts of the sword flew when from behind him, he heard the distinctive sounds of swords being drawn from their sheaths. When he looked behind him, he saw his men crouching low over the ground, cold, determined masks on their faces. Tarragon had no doubt that they meant to meet the attackers emerging from their green cover head on.

Surrounded by his men, Brenn at the front, Tarragon glimpsed a band of men with drawn weapons charging toward them. They looked dirty, thin, and wore ragged clothes. They didn't appear to be well-organized. Some had pitchforks and broken branches, but their shouts echoed throughout the ravine.

Tarragon gripped his hands around the hilt of his sword and made a quick summation of the number of attackers. He and his soldiers were several times outnumbered, and he strove hard not to flinch when Brenn's sword hummed deep as he swung it in defense.

Brenn's voice rose over the confusion. His shouted orders signaled the battle-hardened soldiers to rally behind him. With almost mechanical detachment, the soldiers went on the offensive. It showed their discipline and loyalty to their new commander.

The attackers faltered at the sound of Brenn's voice, and their feet slapped on the frozen earth as they checked their attack. Without thinking about it, Tarragon raised his hand.

Stop!

Everyone stopped in their tracks—even Brenn seemed

confused at the unmistakable authority of the unspoken order. As one, both attackers and defenders turned to look at Tarragon.

Tarragon didn't lower his hand. Instead, he called forth the energies from the sky. In quick response, lightning sliced from overhead and reached down until its sharp tip touched Tarragon's fingers. A blanket of energy enveloped Tarragon, and everyone around shouted in alarm. Even Brenn ducked and took cover, his arms going over his head, his sword still clasped in his hands.

A voice cut through the silence from behind the attackers. "Who are you?" The speaker, a tall, slender, bearded man who looked to be the commander of the ragged band, broke through the ranks. He strode boldly toward Brenn. He paused midway when Brenn's sword dropped before him, barring him from pressing further.

"Steady, Guardian," Tarragon whispered. He watched as the man made a disparaging gesture with his hand.

"What's this? A boy? And what?" The self-professed leader of the attackers hooked his hands on his belt and began to laugh. There was no amusement to the action—rather, it was an expression of mockery. The man scoffed and took a step forward. No longer curious, he craned his neck and made a head count. When he was done, he paused and blinked. "That's it? Are you *it*? You and ten men?"

Head held high, keeping his face expressionless, Tarragon lowered his arm as he watched the leader break into a broad grin.

"This is a fine day, men." The bandit spun around and faced his companions. "What say you? Can we take ten men and a pink-faced boy?"

His men lowered their weapons and leaned on them, their faces breaking into salacious smiles. Even in their relaxed postures, there was no denying their confidence. Tarragon searched into their minds and read that even though their aggression was impressive, most of them were scared and whimpering inside.

The bandit turned once more to Tarragon. "Boy, I trust you and your Guardsman here are ready to surrender. I hope you understand what that means?"

Tarragon made a slow smile and reached out with his mind. *You may be a little bit premature on that assumption, bandit. And there are fifteen men about me, not including me and my Guardian. The two of us are worth double in skills. I'll say we're even.*

The leader's confidence wavered, and he made an uncertain step backward. His men, too, lost their eagerness, and their expressions shifted to one of amazement. Just then, more men drifted out of the woods. Tarragon reached out to them as well, touching their minds and holding them gently in his. The men were curious, for they had never encountered his touch before. They'd only known his father's and brothers'.

Looking back to the leader, Tarragon tightened his grip on the man's mind, but not so tight that it would lose its free will. "What's your name?"

The bandit blinked several times and swallowed hard. "I am called Lucien. Lucien Maia. I do not know you, and yet, I feel and . . . *think* that I should. May I know who I have the honor of addressing?"

"I am Tarragon."

Conflicting expressions played across Lucien's face. Confusion, concern, and then, at last, a consideration. He lifted his sword and gestured its point gently toward Tarragon.

"I felt your father's hold rip from our minds and souls. You are young and without family, prince of the Dacron. Are you looking for survivors?"

Tarragon smiled and fingered the rough leather on the hilt of his sword. "We may be, but I'm not quite sure if your unkempt company will be the right fit." His voice turned peevish. "How sure am I that you are not runners? Cowards who fled the murder of my family so they could save themselves instead? I find it a little convenient to find you here unscathed while my family has been slaughtered like nothing more than garbage."

In his periphery, he saw Brenn's shoulders tense. Showing a disregard of his safety, Tarragon moved until he was standing directly behind Brenn. He touched Brenn's back, as though in a caress, then watched as the bandit's eyes widened in disbelief.

"You see here a lowly soldier who rose in the ranks because of his loyalty to me and skills in command. This one didn't leave my back when everyone around us fell under the attack of the despicable Zaruthran and Caprici soldiers. When my father died, this man experienced the same thing we all did, our souls and minds ripped from our bodies. But this one" — Tarragon ran his hand across Brenn's shoulders and gripped his bicep — "this one didn't run. None of the men you see behind me ran. No, they stayed and rallied themselves to me. They heeded my call without question. Without doubt. You're asking me why they would serve a boy? Why not ask yourself why shouldn't they serve me, a mere boy, as you have claimed. Why didn't they run when you did? Can you answer me that?"

Neither the bandit nor his followers answered him.

With a display of mock regret, Brenn turned his head halfway over his shoulder, his gaze never leaving that of the leader's. "I don't think they can, sire. You more than once proved yourself capable and worthy over every one of us. Why, if it weren't for you, we would all be dead. Instead, we have come back to reclaim your throne."

"Boy, has every reason fled you?" Lucien flung his arms to his sides, his smile defiant. "I salute your plan to recover what you claim is rightfully yours, but I must point out, you're at risk. We have you and your miserable men trapped, and you can die at my orders." He lowered his arms and gave Tarragon a look of mock concern. "Perhaps we can let you leave . . ."

Tarragon inclined his head. "You misunderstood, Lucien." He stepped past Brenn and confronted Lucien face to face. "As the Dacron heir, I have placed myself in this risky position so we might speak."

Lucien glanced at Brenn.

Tarragon noticed that perspiration glistened on Lucien's forehead, despite the cold. Tarragon narrowed his gaze and considered the unnatural flush on the man's cheeks. The man was feverish. Of what illness, Tarragon had to find out.

"I am listening, boy."

The soldiers behind Tarragon crouched down, ready to attack at a moment's notice.

Tarragon caught Lucien's gaze and held it. "Before we speak, I would like you to order your men to lower their . . . weapons . . ." He allowed his voice to linger on the last word. Lucien frowned at his implication but waved a hand. Immediately, his men did as ordered. Perhaps he was not an idiot after all.

CHAPTER SEVEN

Tarragon tilted his head to Brenn, who signaled their ten soldiers do the same, then closed the distance between himself and his lord. Gently, but firmly, he moved Tarragon off to one side and interposed himself between Tarragon and Lucien.

Lucien's gaze narrowed — perhaps he'd registered that the familiarity was allowed without any comment.

"You and your men felt the touch of my mind, and you obeyed without question. For me, that is a clear indication that you *do* recognize my authority. Only a member of the clan Dacron would recognize a Dacron king's touch. If you wish to join me, I will make sure that you and your men are welcome to my protection. If you don't, I really don't mind, as long as you never again set foot on Dacron land or conduct any business within. You have my word that your choice is yours. I will never force you. That would be beyond contempt."

Lucien didn't answer. Instead, he regarded Tarragon, then turned his attention to his men. His brows furrowed as though he was deep in thought.

Tarragon didn't have to read his mind to know what he was thinking. He hadn't missed the scruffy faces surrounding him. Each and every one of them looked undernourished, some scrawny and obviously on the verge of ill health. Despite having been on the road for two months with barely enough food to go around them, Brenn had made sure his men were healthy and clean.

Lucien turned back to Tarragon. Letting out a sigh, he looked down and studied his rusty sword. "Boy, I don't have family left and no house to go home to. My men and I have been together through difficult times, and they will follow my lead. Wherever I lead them." In a quick move, he stepped up to Tarragon and offered up the hilt of his sword. "Sire, I felt your touch, and I cannot deny it soothed me. It is strong and confident and has a surer hold on me than any I've ever felt before. I don't know who you are. We never saw the youngest of the king's children, but you, I will willingly follow." With a stiff bow, he surrendered his blade to Tarragon. It was an act of obeisance that was full of honor and goodwill. Around them, the rest of Lucien's men bowed their heads and surrendered their weapons—even the broken branches were given up.

Brenn tilted his head, and his soldiers stood up and began to collect the weapons. As they did so, Tarragon stepped closer to Lucien. "Is this all of your men, Lucien?"

"No, sire. Most of the men are here, but we have some women and children with us up in the camp deep in the forest. A few more are scattered about. I sent them out yesterday to forage for food. There's another two dozen who are keeping watch in the hills and the forest and roads."

"How many women and children do you have in the camp?"

"Fifty or so, sire. We have some older folk with us, too."

Tarragon made a quick calculation. "There are three dozen here. That means you have roughly about a hundred, hundred fifty men, women, and children with you."

"Around that number, yes, sire."

"How many of those who are here now have military backgrounds?" When Lucien started to speak up, Tarragon gripped his shoulder and looked at the men. "No, Lucien, let them speak for themselves."

Of the three dozen men who had attacked them earlier, almost all raised their hands, save for six. Tarragon smiled in encouragement. "What of you six, what background do you have?"

One by one, each man shouted their backgrounds.

"Cook!"

"Medic!"

"Gardener!"

"Engineer!"

"Blacksmith!"

When one of the men didn't answer, Tarragon curled his finger at him to come closer.

The burly man stepped forward. "Sire, I am a criminal. When the Zaruthran soldiers came and attacked Dacron palace, I escaped my prison and fled. I followed Lucien."

"And what was your crime?"

"I was a farmer, but when the war started, I had no one to rely on to harvest the fields. Everyone was sent out to join the army called by the king. Without harvest, I had no money, and I failed to pay the taxes."

Tarragon didn't immediately reply, but he regarded Lucien's men. Most had sat down cross-legged and now looked in his direction. Others remained standing but appeared to be relaxed. They, too, were looking at him in silence, waiting for his next decision.

Brenn walked up beside him to flank his side. He still held his sword, ever vigilant and on guard. Reaching a decision, Tarragon drew in a breath and raised his voice so everyone would hear him.

"Listen to me. I am Tarragon. I am the last heir to the Dacron. It was my mind that held your will earlier, the mind that gave you an order not to attack me and my mine. You obeyed me then. Now I ask you to listen to what I am about to say.

"For all intents, you are all criminals, for you ran from your duties. But I understand why you ran. I, myself, ordered my men to retreat from the attacking forces of the Zaruthrans and Capricis. It was a decision not made out of cowardice but out of self-preservation. Either we retreated, or we died. The choice was clear. We wanted to live. We came back to Dacron Palace thinking that we would be able to rally more forces to defend our land and families, but we were met with tragedy. The Zaruthrans and Capricis did much damage to us and murdered not only my family, but everyone else who were innocents to the ploys of their politics.

"I know not why they have such anger toward me and my family, our clan, but they do, and they are not going to stop killing us until the last of the Dacron line has been eradicated. I will not allow that. *We* will not allow that.

"We have the winter to hide in. No one can cross the paths to the palace this time of the year. We have six months to rally and fortify.

"I need you to come back to our land, to the palace, and take service there. Who comes with me?"

For a moment, no one answered his call, but then, order vanished, and everyone started speaking at once.

A voice cut through the confusion. "What if I choose not to follow you, will you have me killed?"

Tarragon shook his head. "No. As I've said before, I will never force anyone to serve me or to join the clan."

The same voice spoke up. This time, the speaker stood up. "Your father held us with contempt and pressed his intent when we didn't want to follow. Are you going to do the same?"

"No. As I've said before, I will not hold your wills prisoner. It is against my conscience and my ruling for a king to hold the clan's mind as prisoner. That was not the purpose of this talent. It is here to give you guidance, to keep the peace and the calm. To help you reach the right decision you choose."

"But your father —"

"My father was wrong, and his actions partly caused this war. I wish to end the war and to make peace. My goal is to unite Oryon under one rule, one king. That way, everyone will benefit from the peace."

"Even the mages?"

Tarragon turned a surprised look toward Brenn. He had never expected him to say that. For the second time, Tarragon wondered about Brenn's background. His violet eyes were rare, and the sword he now carried was advanced technology. For a lowly soldier, Brenn hadn't looked surprised when Tarragon had displayed his power. Instead, he'd looked relieved.

"It is also my goal to find the mages, wherever they may be, and ask them to join our cause."

The silence became oppressive, as though charged with electricity. Men shifted, restless and troubled. Talk of mages always had that effect on people. Tarragon sensed their fear, for what he was proposing was going to change their fundamental thinking and culture.

"I know you are afraid of the mages, but let me ask you this, why are you afraid? What is it that they have done that causes you to be threatened?"

No one answered him. Expressions of hope warred with those of the skeptical.

"The mages chose to leave and live off in secret because we feared them, and yet nothing in our history has ever recorded that they harmed anyone. There is not a single record of a mage caught killing or murdering or causing war. It was men who did that, not the mages. Even now, they are not with us, and the Zaruthrans and the Capricis seek our destruction."

Tarragon reached out with his mind and touched each and every man's mind, soothing their fears away, raising their hopes. He raised his hand and allowed the magic to flow onto it. Slowly, tentatively, the blue current spread over his hand and fingers, gathering in a ball at the palm of his hand. Many men exclaimed, astonished to find a mage among them.

"How did you think the Dacron continued to hold the clan minds together? Other than my father, were the past kings not kind and gentle with you?"

Tarragon smiled and played with the ball of electricity in his hand. "This magic in me—it has long been dormant, but it is what saved us when the enemy ambushed us in the mountains. It was this magic that enabled me to keep my men safe. It was in the absence of this that I failed you."

The farmer who had turned criminal stood up. "If it was your magic that saved you all, and the magic I feel in my mind and soul, then I will follow you, sire. Your touch is gentle, and I have felt the minds of two kings in my lifetime. Your father's was strong, but yours is stronger, and yet I feel a trust in it. I feel that you love our clan. I sense that you would do everything in your power and capability to re-build our strength." The man bowed his head, his fist to his chest. "I follow you, sire. You have my life to use as you see fit."

"I promise you that I will die to protect my clan," Tarragon answered.

Brenn bowed his head and placed his fist to his chest.

Formally, Tarragon nodded.

Brenn straightened. He looked at each man and raised his voice. "Tarragon!"

The forest rang with the voices of those who answered his call. Tarragon's name echoed throughout the clearing. He had no doubt that those still in the forest would hear them.

Lucien stepped up to him, his face reflecting surprise and jubilance. "Boy, you are an astonishing young man. You are also generous to a fault, and that may be your weakness. Also, your left knee is wobbling, and if I were an enemy, I would have taken you down. I offer to you my services, sire. I was once a combat trainer under your father's command. I will have to come out of retirement and teach you a thing or two to defend yourself. The old king was wrong to have kept you from training."

Tarragon's grin broke widely, followed by laughter. "Thank you, Lucien. I thought you looked familiar, but you left the palace when I was much younger, so I wasn't sure. Thank you. I would need your services."

"I gave my oath, and I will fulfill them. Now" — he pointed his thumb over his shoulder toward Brenn's back — "what are you going to do with that mage Guardian of yours?"

CHAPTER EIGHT

Darkness had settled by the time they'd returned. Everywhere, the wind howled, and the snow flurried wildly. Under the artificial glow of lights blazing from the posts standing along the walls surrounding the vast estate, Tarragon saw some twenty or so men standing in attention. Most of them leaned on crutches, but the swords by their sides and their grim faces betrayed their seeming helplessness. As Tarragon and his retinue neared the gates, the group before them parted to give way to a man who walked between them. The man began to distribute bowls, which the soldiers received with thanks. A few of the more able soldiers set their bowls aside and saluted Tarragon when he and his group stopped before them. The rest continued to eat, but their eyes were wary, their gazes on the new faces following Tarragon.

Tarragon glanced at Brenn, who had guided his *septurecce* alongside his before getting off the beast. He extended a helping hand to assist Tarragon down, but before Tarragon could offer a snarky remark, Brenn bowed his head and took the reins from his fingers.

"Sire, I would advise that you announce that we are accompanied by worthy men. Well, at least, as worthy as we assume them to be. Explain to them that the newcomers are gladly following you and will enter your service."

The words were spoken so low that only Tarragon heard, but still, he felt his cheeks heat in embarrassment. He should really pay more attention to what was going on. Thank the

Goddess Brenn had more insight than he did.

Brenn dipped his head, stepped aside and gestured to one of the men. Two men moved quickly to join them. One of them took the reins from Brenn's hand and led the beasts away while the other listened as Brenn gave him instructions. Tarragon turned to Lucien and waved him over. When Lucien stepped near, Tarragon pointed to where Brenn stood.

"Tell the men to trust Brenn's man here and follow him to where you are to settle. Tell them to get some food and rest. I'll have the medic go over and check on the injured and sick. We will have to go back for the women and children tomorrow, after you've rested."

Lucien flashed a rakish smile. "Sire, I'm not a humble man, and neither are my men. We have lived as bandits for some time now. We know how to take care of ourselves."

"Good. As I said, as soon as you're ready, we'll fetch the rest of your people and bring them here. Assure them that they will be safe here. For the time being."

"Tradition dictates we have three years to recuperate. That will give me enough time to recruit more men."

"Define *more*, Lucien."

Lucien grinned widely. "How many do you want me to get for you?"

"A thousand. Two would be better. Ten would be best."

"Ahh . . ." Lucien scratched his head and grew thoughtful. "That's going to take me more than a few months to accomplish, sire."

"And here I thought you were a mage," Tarragon said.

Lucien's hand dropped to his side, and he paled even as his eyes grew wider.

"I didn't say I was one, sire. I said Brenn was." He pointed over his shoulder toward Brenn with his thumb.

Tarragon grinned. He couldn't seem to stop himself from

teasing the brigand. "Legend says that only a mage can tell who is one."

"It's the eyes, sire. Mages have violet eyes." Lucien's eyes grew wider his shoulders stiffened.

"I haven't heard of that one yet."

"You hear it now." Lucien looked to where Brenn stood. "Sire, I will do as you ask and look for more men and women to recruit. You're asking for a miracle, but you standing here, alive and out of reach from your enemies, is a miracle by itself. Who am I to question the Goddess' purpose?"

Tarragon didn't respond. Instead, he signaled to Brenn.

The Guardian came over immediately and gave him a salute, but his gaze went toward Lucien.

"Can you find some men to go with Lucien? Once Derek clears him, he'll be leaving to get the rest of his people and begin his search for more recruits." Tarragon regarded the former bandit. "Choose from those whom you trust among your men and also those that Brenn recommends. Spending time together on the road will either make you kill each other or make you bond. Remember. We were all targeted by the Zaruthrans and the Capricis. We share a common enemy. Together, we can convince more people to come over to our side." Tarragon turned to go, but then faced Lucien again. "Just make sure you don't get into too much trouble should our enemies hear of our plans."

Lucien's grin broadened. "I think I can handle a few troublemakers, sire. I forgot to tell you I was a decorated soldier in my youth."

Tarragon regarded him, thinking that he had stumbled into someone he instinctively trusted. "I'm sure you can, Lucien. Do me a favor, though?"

"Anything, sire."

"Come back in one piece?"

"I intend to, sire. The Zaruthrans and Capricis have a lot

to answer for, and I intend to be there when they do." Lucien struck his fist to his chest and dipped his head low. He glanced up at Brenn and gave him a brief nod before turning around to lead his men to where a soldier pointed them.

By the time Tarragon entered his rooms, he was ready to tear the clothes off his back. They felt grimy and itchy, but he was too tired to move any faster other than to sit on the edge of his bed and slowly unbutton his shirt. He tried to take it off and cursed out loud when he couldn't, only to realize he'd forgotten to take off his heavy coat. Chuckling at himself, he shrugged the shirt back over his shoulders and pulled on the jacket. Finally freed of the bulk, he gratefully took off the offending shirt. Next, he began to remove his shoes and socks. After toeing them off, he looked down at his trousers and thought that he didn't have to take them off. But then his crotch began to itch, and he had no choice but to stand and take those off as well.

"Having a hard time?"

Tarragon looked up and saw Brenn leaning against the door jamb.

"Can you help me out?"

Brenn shook his head, but there was an indulgent smile on his lips. "You're helpless without a body servant. We should find one for you."

"No. I have you, remember? You do very well helping me in and out of my clothes." Tarragon grinned when one of Brenn's brows rose. "You're also quite good at giving me a bath."

Brenn shook his head once more before going across the room to open the door to the bathing room. "Get in here. You stink."

"Oh, now I stink. Good to know, oh Guardian."

Tarragon walked into the shower and waved a hand under the control panel. "I wish I weren't so tired."

"Don't slip," Brenn cautioned from behind him.

Tarragon ignored him, but he did as he was told. As he soaped his body clean, he wondered about how he'd managed to stay upright only that morning.

When he stepped out, he didn't see Brenn anywhere, so he went ahead and dried himself. Still naked, he slipped under the covers and closed his eyes.

The bed dipped. Startled, Tarragon opened his eyes only to see Brenn get in beside him. He was naked.

"I'm sorry I woke you," he whispered.

"Where were you?"

"I checked on Lucien and his men. They're fed and have settled in their rooms."

"I hope I didn't make a mistake," Tarragon said.

"I don't think you did. You saw into their minds and gained their trust. That's not such an easy thing to do, not with men like Lucien."

Tarragon yawned and slid up closer until his body lay beside Brenn. He wrapped his arm over Brenn's stomach and laid his head on his chest. He stayed like that for a long minute, listening to the steady rhythm of the heart beating. He stole a glance up at Brenn, seeing his eyes closed.

Brenn was so handsome, but for Tarragon, it was his eyes that sealed the deal for him. The way they watched him. The way they crinkled at the sides whenever he was laughing. The indulgence in them whenever he thought Tarragon was acting less than the king he was supposed to be. He still didn't know much about Brenn's background, but he had no doubt that his people trusted him, and so did Tarragon. The war had erased societal barriers, and he found that he didn't care what Brenn's background was.

He inched up until he was high enough that he could cup one side of Brenn's face, then pulled him closer until their mouths met. With no hesitation, Brenn moved his hand down Tarragon's waist. When Brenn's lips moved against Tarragon, there was no need to think twice. Tarragon deepened the kiss, pressing his body closer until he felt the growing arousal push against his own. A moan vibrated against their lips, but Tarragon had no idea who it came from. Tarragon didn't care. He rocked against Brenn, letting his body speak for him.

Brenn got the message and somehow managed to pull Tarragon further up until he was able to put his fingers inside Tarragon, making him hiss in pleasure. His entrance was still loose from their activity earlier, and he widened his legs, dropping them on either side of Brenn's hips, to allow those fingers farther inside him. Brenn shifted their bodies until Tarragon lay flush on the bed on his stomach. Tarragon dropped his head into his outstretched arms, angling his body and raising himself on his knees so his butt raised off the bed. There was no need to wait long. Soon the fingers disappeared, only to return, this time oily and digging deeper inside him. When he thought he could stand the wait no longer, he felt Brenn slowly sink into his body, making Tarragon release a relieved breath. The familiar length filled him just like it had earlier, only this time, he didn't need to be afraid he'd slip and fall.

Wanting something more than what he was getting, Tarragon rolled his hips, making Brenn grunt in response and still his movements. Brenn moved away only to return, his thrust a movement of fluidity that took Tarragon's breath away. He gasped out loud, reaching back so he could hold onto Brenn's waist.

The minutes passed — maybe they were hours, Brenn slid in and out of Tarragon in an endless passionate embrace that didn't seem to stop. Finally, Tarragon felt Brenn jerk hard against him. When the rush of heat filled him to overflowing limits, Tarragon shot his own load on the sheets beneath him.

If there had ever been any doubts in his mind, Tarragon knew at that instant, he could never let Brenn go. Ever.

CHAPTER NINE

A week after their return to the palace, Tarragon pondered how they were going to survive the winter as he ate his breakfast. Although it was hot and delicious, he was quite aware that the offering was meager and not what he was used to being served at the palace. The food before them was the same choice they'd had during their trek through the mountain pass. After months of eating the same thing, Tarragon was tired of it. They were in sore need to replenish their supplies, but with the weather turning, he knew they wouldn't have much luck anytime soon. Already, the wind howled outside the floor-to-ceiling windows lining one side of the room. He looked at the men sitting around the table, and a smile curled on his lips. If his father were still alive, he'd have whipped Tarragon's butt for daring to ask commoners to join a royal at breakfast. Well, his father was no longer around, and he'd never really understood the logic of the man's scorn toward those he deemed beneath his station.

To his right sat Brenn. His Guardian sat ramrod straight in his chair and kept sending glaring glances toward Lucien, who sat opposite him. Derek sat opposite Tarragon. Of the three men, it was Derek whom Tarragon found most puzzling. He didn't even know why he'd invited Derek to join them, but something had pushed him to do so. For some odd reason, he kept thinking that Derek was a man who should be in his inner circle. Other than Brenn, who had hardly taken a bite of his food from all the glares he was sending Lucien, all of them were quietly eating their food.

A slight breeze caused Tarragon to turn around and peer at the windows behind him. He glanced back when Brenn quietly put down his utensils and stood up, then began checking each of the windows. He didn't seem to find anything wrong until he reached the window at the farthest end. Brenn opened it and checked its hinges before closing it firmly.

"It seems secure for now, but I'll have one of the men check on it again," Brenn said as he walked back to the table. He shivered as he sat down, blowing into the palm of his hands and rubbed them together to warm them. "We'll need more firewood in this place if we're to survive the winter here."

"Oh, if only we had one of those heating machines, we wouldn't have to send men out in the cold," Derek said wistfully.

"What heating machine?" Tarragon looked directly at Derek.

Derek's face became animated. "When I was a little boy, my family spent some time in the west. Come wintertime, it was our custom to go back to my mother's family home. The house had no fireplaces, but it was always warm."

"No need for firewood?" Lucien asked, his face reflecting the same confusion Tarragon felt.

"Yes, no firewood. All we had to do was go to the basement and turn on this machine. It ran on electricity and only took about an hour to heat up the whole place. And that place was a small palace."

"That's incredible," Tarragon said. "I wonder how we can get that kind of technology for over here." He looked about him. "I love my home, but it gets too cold in winter. Like you, we, too, used to travel to our southern home. Unfortunately, we can't travel there."

"Not yet, anyway," Brenn said.

Tarragon sent him a small smile. No. They could not afford going south. He could not risk taking his men across the country to go east.

"Well, if you want, you can always send me to Oflor. I'm still in contact with my relatives there. I'm sure they can sell it to me for a reasonable price, and they won't ask questions. Not too many, I hope. They knew my mother." Derek paused when he saw Tarragon's amused smile. "Uhm, she was a daughter of the House Kayel."

"Hmm, I've heard of that family before," Lucien said thoughtfully as he chewed on a piece of rehydrated fruit. "Aren't their estates somewhere around the Drumdour Mountains?"

"Yes, that's the place," Derek said with a broad smile. "You know of it?"

Lucien didn't answer immediately. He chewed thoughtfully before looking at Derek.

Tarragon couldn't quite interpret his expression, and he didn't want to dip into Lucien's mind.

After a while, Lucien smiled and began to slice the meat on his plate. "It's commonly known among the people there that the Drumdour Mountain range bordering the estates is where a community of mages supposedly resides."

When Derek didn't reply, Tarragon looked at him. "Is what Lucien saying true? Have you heard of this talk of mages?"

After a moment's hesitation, Derek nodded. His cheeks flushed red. "Yes, sire. I had heard the same thing."

His mind whirling, Tarragon blinked down at his food. Like Lucien, he, too, picked up his knife and fork began to cut the slice of meat on his plate. "Tell me, how is it that their presence there is known and yet I have never heard of anyone mentioning it before?"

Derek threw a nervous glance toward Brenn. He cleared

his throat before answering and looked back at Tarragon. "According to my friends—please remember, this was way back when I was only ten or twelve years—the Lord's family enjoyed a kinship with the mages. From what I learned of the history my mother told me, the Lord of that time, Oornach, offered that part of the estates as a refuge for all mages when they were thrown out of their homes."

"How is it that my father or my brothers never mentioned this to me? I do remember how my brothers spent a lot of their time trying to search for the mages' hideout. They never found them, of course. It was as if the mages never existed." Tarragon placed his elbows on the table, his food forgotten.

Lucien made a negative gesture with his hand. "The house of Kayel is headed by academic men. I remember reading about Lord Oornach. He never publicly denounced the mages when the rest of the families of Oryon did. It wouldn't surprise me if he'd invited them over to his estates and gave them refuge. According to the records, he was quiet and allowed very few guests to visit. His children were also academically inclined and would join their parent in the laboratories."

"What do they do in those laboratories?" Tarragon asked Derek.

Derek shrugged. "I have no idea. I didn't really go near the buildings where they worked. However, my father once told me that the Kayels made their fortune from their inventions."

Tarragon was instantly interested. "Technology. You're talking about the family that invented the electric generator." He glanced from Brenn to Lucien. Brenn's face remained stoic, but Lucien's grin was broader than ever.

"Derek, do you think you can find out what they were working on? Also, I need to know if they are our supporters or lean toward our enemies."

Derek's smirked. "Oh, I think you would be surprised to know who they supported, sire. I know for a fact the Kayels are a peace-loving family. However, I can still remember the weapons their guards carried back when I was a boy. I can honestly say they do not like sharing their technology. It surprised me that they sold your brother the generators and taught him how to make more of them. I also know that my mother hated the Zaruthrans. According to her, her hatred for them is shared by all of the Kayels." He glanced at Lucien. "It is also a well-known fact that someone of the lord's family suffered under the hands of one of those princes."

"Now that piece of information I didn't know about. What happened?" Lucien asked.

"She died." Derek raised a brow, his expression meaningful.

Tarragon nodded quietly. He didn't need for Derek to elaborate. Knowing the cruel nature of the Zaruthrans, the poor woman must have suffered horribly.

Tarragon set aside his utensils and pushed back his chair. When the others did the same, he waved them back. "No, don't stop eating on account of me. Goddess, this is exciting news." He began to pace the floor. "If what you're saying is true, then, Lucien, I need you to postpone your trip. You can assign someone else to go find more recruits. Going to Oflor is more important. I need to get there before our enemy does."

Lucien didn't disagree. "If you can give me a little time, sire, I can go now, back to the mountains, and instruct my son to take over the job you asked of me before I join you. That should not take me more than three days. Once you're successful in convincing the Kayels to join your cause, I can rejoin my men."

"Yes, that's a good plan." Tarragon hadn't known that

Lucien had a son. The man's mind was not as open as he'd first thought, but he could barely contain his excitement and decided to forget about it for the time being. Thoughts of gaining the mages' trust eclipsed everything else. To have the mages by his side would be something his enemies would never expect.

From what little education he had regarding the mages, he knew they had been loyal and fierce allies to their clans before they had been subjected to bigotry and fear. Deep inside, Tarragon knew that without the mages by their side, he would not last the year. Historically, wars had been fought and won with the mages always on the winning side. It was right they were to be feared—they were that powerful. But now they were not even recognized as citizens of Oryon. It was time to change things around.

And then there was the matter of the technology. His affinity with the generators they'd had to leave in the mountains during their flight back to Dacron Palace was something he couldn't ignore. Somehow, he knew that if he could get his hands on more machines, he could do more with his talent.

Tarragon would need to convince both the House Kayel and the mages they protected to join his clan. If he failed, and his enemies discovered the mages' location, then representatives from other kingdoms would come and offer the mages empty promises. Most likely, the Zaruthrans would swoop down and kill every Kayel, down to their innocent children, just to force the mages to join their side.

Gaining the trust of a technologically inclined family and the mages they protected would be a gift from the Goddess. The mages might be spurned by the Zaruthrans and Capricis, but as he was most likely part mage, he was sure that they could become a fierce ally.

Tarragon turned to Brenn. "Have your men ready themselves. Lucien will start the journey to talk to his son and join us back here before noon. We leave in three days."

Chapter Ten

Tarragon's excitement and impatience grew as the days passed. After promising to join him and Brenn in three days, Lucien, accompanied by his and Brenn's most trusted men, left to get the rest of those he'd left behind in their forest encampment. Events were moving fast, although Tarragon saw the doubt in Brenn's eyes. Or was it hesitation? He didn't really want to read into his Guardian's mind, but he knew he would have to, sooner rather than later. He would need to ask the difficult questions. Brenn had offered no opinion on Tarragon's and Lucien's plan, but he had not offered any objections, either. Lucien's comment before, that Brenn was a mage, bothered Tarragon because of his lack of reaction. Another issue that bothered him was Brenn's refusal to sleep with him while they were on the road. He knew it was because they were traveling and Brenn wanted to keep his men's morale up, but surely, no one would think it strange for Brenn to sleep in Tarragon's tent? He didn't doubt everyone knew Brenn slept with him every night at the palace, so why the sudden proprietary measures? Tarragon decided to leave things for now. He had more pressing issues to focus on. Also, he didn't know how to approach his deepening feelings for his Guardian.

On the third day since finding out about the mage's hideout, Tarragon and his retinue secretly hurried along the back-country trails. Tarragon rode on his beast dressed in thick, warm clothing and fur-lined boots. Each day they traveled, Tarragon reached out with his mind to monitor for any signs of fear or strain on his accompanying soldiers. He knew that Brenn kept everyone in line, and he doubted his soldiers would ever lose discipline in his presence.

However, he did hear the quiet conversations around the campfire after he bade them a good night and entered the solace of his tent. There were the occasional banter and jokes, but mostly, the men kept silent. Tarragon knew it was because they were, by now, aware that they were heading to look for the mages. Tradition was a hard thing to break, and fearing the mages had become a tradition of sorts. In the three days they'd been traveling, it had become a habit for Tarragon to send out soothing thoughts to his men. It was the nights that were the most difficult for him, though, since he slept alone. By the end of the third day, Brenn followed Tarragon into his tent. Unfortunately, it was not to join him there, but to discuss with Tarragon his plans.

"Sire, I suggest you rest now. Whether or not Lucien comes by midnight, I'm planning to move our position to avoid detection."

"Why? Do you think our enemies have detected our movements?"

"They think you dead, sire, so no. I don't think they have. However, it is best to move in darkness from now on. We are entering into neighboring lands, and we'll be more likely to get seen and questioned by patrol soldiers from those estates. It would be wiser to keep our presence unknown and avoid all manner of contact. Even a minor lord would be suspicious of unknown travelers and strike at us. Times are hard, and the war has made many fear the presence of strangers."

Tarragon nodded. He saw the logic in Brenn's plan. "I don't think we have any other choice. All right, we'll do as you say. Just make sure to give Lucien the chance to reach us. He still has four hours before his deadline."

"Oh, I'm not worried that Lucien will join us."

"What are you worried about, then?"

"The lordlings of this area. We have no idea whose side they are on."

"Agreed. All right, let me have my rest, Guardian."

"Sleep well, sire," Brenn said with a slight bow. He turned to exit the tent when Tarragon reached out to grip his arm.

"Stay."

Brenn looked up to meet Tarragon's gaze. Though it was intense, there was a gentleness to his eyes that warmed Tarragon's heard. "I can't. Not when I'm doing my best to keep you alive."

"So, it's not because . . ."

"No, sire. Rest assured, we will have our time together. I feel it is something we both want. But now is not the time. We are on a dangerous mission, and I need to focus on keeping you safe."

Tarragon let out a sigh and rubbed his palm on Brenn's arm. "Go then. Do your duty, Guardian."

"Always," Brenn said, holding Tarragon's gaze in his. Another brief bow, and he left the tent.

Tarragon knew he should not press Brenn into something that went beyond their relationship as king and Guardian, but he couldn't help it. He hadn't felt safe in anyone's presence for the longest time, and he craved it. He didn't know where their relationship would lead them, either, but he really wanted it to be more than the intimate, though platonic one that they now shared since they'd started traveling.

Fatigue descended on him then, and he let out a wide yawn. His pallet beckoned to him, and he was not about to refuse its call. He only had a few hours to rid himself of his exhaustion before he would be wakened for more traveling.

Not bothering to take off his clothes, he lay on the pallet and closed his eyes.

"Sire, it's time."

Tarragon jerked awake to see Brenn's tall shadowed form bending over him. Blinking his weariness away, he sat up and took Brenn's offered arm. He pulled himself up to his feet, then let out another yawn.

"Has Lucien come?"

Brenn took a step back, his gaze running over Tarragon. It was as though he were inspecting Tarragon's body for signs of weakness. "Yes. He came in an hour ago. He brought with him fifty men."

Tarragon nodded sleepily and stretched his arms up. "All right, give me a few minutes, and then we should leave."

By the time he joined Brenn and Lucien by the fire, the soldiers had dismantled his tent and loaded his things on the cart that carried most of their supplies. Brenn approached him with a plate of cold rations, which Tarragon accepted gratefully. He studied Brenn's and Lucien's faces. Both men looked tired, but then that was not unexpected. However, he sensed the tension in the air and that worried him.

"What has happened? What am I missing?" When neither man answered, Tarragon pushed with his mind. "Talk to me."

Lucien directed a look toward Brenn before facing Tarragon.

"I was just telling Brenn here that I and my men crossed five estates to get here. All five were well guarded, and they saw us plain as day. Yet, none of them sounded any alarm. My men are skilled, but we're not so extraordinary as to be virtually invisible. Unless those soldiers were so untrained they couldn't discern sand and wind from men moving only a few yards in front of them."

Tarragon frowned, confused. "What are you saying, exactly? That they didn't see you?"

"Sire, I went up to a gate and danced the jig, and they didn't see me."

Tarragon blinked. "I don't understand."

"He's implying that a mage covered him and his men from the guards," Brenn said.

"And what else could it have been?" Lucien rounded on Brenn. "Why don't you just admit it, Guardian? Admit that somehow, *you* managed to send word to your kin, and they cast a spell on our presence."

Brenn rolled his eyes. "Let's say what you're saying is true. How was I supposed to do that?"

"Well . . . you . . . you . . ." Lucien stuttered, apparently at a loss for words. He fell silent and glared at Brenn. "I don't know! *You* tell us!"

"This is stupid." Brenn crossed his arms in front of him.

"I am not stupid!" Lucien's face had turned a startling shade between purple and red. Tarragon couldn't really tell, because the firelight was too dim for him to make sure. But enough was enough. When Brenn raised a condescending brow, Lucien growled deep in his throat.

Tarragon put up his palm. "Quiet. Both of you."

Both men glared at each other before turning his direction. "Lucien? Why are you so afraid of the thought of mages protecting you? You have seen my abilities and are not afraid of me. And you, Brenn. Why are you goading Lucien so? And you have not addressed his questions once."

Instead of answering, both Brenn and Lucien tightened their lips and didn't respond.

Tarragon let out a sigh. "All right. I know you both have your problems with each other, but I can sense you're both loyal to me. If you don't want to answer my questions now, I expect you to come to me and speak your minds later. I won't tolerate your personal opinions of each other affecting our goal. We need to find those mages and get them to our side. Knowing the Zaruthrans and Capricis, they will most likely be searching for them like we are. Unlike me, however, who only want them to get out of their self-imposed exile, our enemies won't hesitate to line them up and order their deaths."

"But—" Lucien began, but Tarragon flashed him a frown.

"If indeed the mages cast a spell to protect your presence, then accept it with good grace. I'm sure the mages know we are coming and if, by their actions, they seem to be protective of us, then take it with grace and don't deny them. Be glad they are appearing to take our side. You can ask your questions once we find them and they've joined our ranks. Understood?"

Lucien pursed his lips and gave a brief not. "Understood."

"And will you please stop challenging Brenn whether he is a mage or not? *I* am not asking. I am not going to bother to ask. I made him my Guardian without knowing his background. All I know is that I trust him. Like I trust you, for some reason."

"Thank you, sire," Brenn said.

"As for you." Tarragon faced Brenn. "Only when you're ready will you tell me. I expect nothing less."

"Understood, sire," Brenn said without meeting his gaze.

When Lucien opened his mouth to say something, Tarragon sent him a glare of his own. Instantly, Lucien's mouth snapped closed.

"I'll go get the men ready. We should move out," Lucien bit out.

"Thank you," Tarragon said.

Lucien walked away, but he wasn't done. "Although, I'm wondering at the logic of moving about in darkness. I mean, we're practically invisible, thanks to the mages, whether they admit it or not."

"Lucien?" Tarragon called out.

Lucien turned around, his expression innocent. "Yes, sire."

"Please be quiet."

Lucien flashed him a broad grin. "Quiet as a mouse!"

Tarragon shook his head. Lucien was proving to be an impertinent man, but he was also kind of funny. He laughed low in his chest and turned to Brenn. His Guardian's face was impassive, and Tarragon sensed his unease. However, he didn't want to force Brenn to reveal his background soon.

"Shall we move out, Guardian?" Tarragon finally asked.

Brenn inclined his head. "Five minutes, sire."

Tarragon smiled to hide his frustration — and amusement. He wanted to laugh and cry at the same time. And scream at the men. But he couldn't do that. He felt as though he had won a small victory. He had never thought he would be in a situation where he would play the elder to two mature men. For Goddess' sake, he was only eighteen!

"We have a lot to discuss when we get home, Brenn. You and Lucien have a lot of things to tell me." He watched as Brenn bowed his head and moved to join Lucien and the rest of their company. Looking at the newcomers, Tarragon released a relieved breath. He had never doubted Lucien and his capability. But seeing the additional fifty men was evidence of the man's ability to recruit. Suddenly his exhaustion no longer bothered him. He looked forward to finding the mages. For the first time in a very long while, he felt the hope that he'd given his people. The future looked brighter.

CHAPTER ELEVEN

They traveled in darkness, the wind bitingly cold. Tarragon pulled the cape tighter around himself and let out a sigh. Although no one complained, he knew that the others were just as miserable as he was. The lowland plains and the patchwork of paddies and creeks lay frozen before him, the ground, hard and slippery in places. He wasn't worried. The elegant and calm *septurecce* with their six legs were sure-footed and ensured his safety. It was one of the many reasons why they were favored by Tarragon's family. Not only did their long, dense undercoat and coarse outer coat provide the warmth for both beast and rider, for its coat was highly resistant to soaking rain, keeping the beast warm in much lower temperatures than they were now experiencing. They also were extremely loyal beasts. They didn't need to be broken to be ridden. They were gentle working beasts that were very easy to care for. That was, if they liked their caretakers. If they didn't, they made their dissatisfaction known with their six feet and large hooves. As far as Tarragon knew, it was only his family that bred the animals. Because of the war, they had so few left.

He wondered if the House of Kayel had any technology that would make it possible to breed and protect the animals. He leaned down, dug his fingers into the coat and let out a sigh of relief. The warmth from the fur gave life once more to his numbed fingers. When he crooked his fingers deeper, the *septurecce* made a clicking sound. Tarragon looked up and met the blue-eyed gaze. He smiled and leaned further forward until his chest lay on the beast's back. Once more, the *septurecce* clicked and huffed, but continued on its way.

Tarragon wondered as he lay there, feeling his torso gradually thaw. On a whim, he reached out tentatively, hoping he was right, that the beast had more to its mind than he'd been led to believe. What met his mind was a curiosity that bordered on the edge of amusement. Tarragon blinked. He hadn't expected that. Feeling the exhaustion creeping into his muscles, Tarragon allowed his mind to drift from the worries of the day. Instead of worrying about what might or might not happen, he turned his gaze to observe his surroundings.

The trees wore the dejected look of winter, looking old, wild, and neglected. But then, when one looked closely, there was life in them. The bright buds of winter flowers broke through, stark contrasts to the whites and grays that came with the season. It was only then that Tarragon realized that the first rays of sunrise were falling across the trail before them. Up ahead, the trees thickened into woodlands, and deeper still lay a dense forest.

The sound of galloping hooves made Tarragon raise his head. He watched as Brenn pulled in beside him, slowing down his beast until they were side by side.

"Sire, we've reached the border of Oflor. Lucien's up ahead, scouting for a trail to cut across without being seen."

"I thought he said we were virtually invisible?"

Brenn didn't reply, merely narrowed his eyes on Tarragon, expressionless.

Tarragon laughed and straightened. "Don't be such a grouch. Now, where is this trail you're talking about?"

Brenn pointed into the forest. "Through there."

Tarragon frowned in the direction and saw nothing but trees and more trees. "Are you sure? That doesn't look like the easy path you're claiming it to be."

"The woods get thinner further on. Once we're through that, there should be a meadowed valley, and once we cross that, we will have reached the estates of the Kayels."

"For someone who supposedly doesn't know anything about the Kayels or this province, you sure sound like you're more than familiar with this place."

Brenn's cheek muscles tightened briefly before he threw Tarragon a telling glance. "Do you think your family has a treaty with the Kayels? Maybe something your father forgot to mention to you?"

Tarragon grinned at the obvious snub to his comment, but he let it alone. He would dig it out of Brenn, and when that time came, he would have all the answers. He'd make sure of it. For now, he thought about the question, once more regretting the collective memories of his family were lost for all time.

"I wouldn't know. Father never so much as thought to include me in his thoughts or activities."

"We could sure use that knowledge now," Brenn complained.

"I know what you mean, but that's all under the rug. What we need to do is to get to the Lord and talk to him before our enemies can. I need his alliance, and any information about where and how to find the mages would be of great advantage to us."

"Maybe they can teach you more about your abilities."

Tarragon threw a glance at Brenn and was met with an innocent look.

"What? Do you think no one's noticed your talents? Sire, you saved us all because of that talent. That secret's long been discovered."

"I know you all know or have seen my abilities. But to your question, yes, that's one of my motives. I know I need to know how to control this talent. What if I use it the wrong way?"

Brenn smiled gently. "I highly doubt that, sire."

"Why? You trust me enough?"

"No. Not that."

"Then why? What is it?"

"We've all felt your father's touch in our minds, sire. Let me assure you, you're nothing like your father or brothers, sire. You, Tarragon, have a gentle, loving touch." With a last smile to Tarragon, Brenn signaled his beast to a canter, leaving Tarragon to stare after him in amazement.

He was still staring after Brenn when Lucien rode up next to him.

"Sire, we're going to go through that forest there. Once we're beyond it, we should reach Oflor."

Tarragon nodded, still gazing after Brenn's retreating back. "I know. Brenn told me."

"He did? Hmm, for someone who claims he knows nothing about this place, he sure knows a lot about it."

Tarragon threw Lucien a glance and was met with his broad grin. "Funny you should say that."

"Why? Have you finally realized that your Guardian's more than he's pretending to be?"

"And what if he is, Lucien? Will you hold it against him?"

"Nah," Lucien said, letting out a sigh. His breath froze in the air and his face blurred from the thickness of the fog. "It'll just prove that he's a man of many secrets." He looked behind him to the men following in their wake. "We all have our secrets, sire. Nothing wrong about that."

Tarragon waited for Lucien to continue, but Lucien stayed silent. They rode on for several more minutes until Brenn rode up to join them.

"We're here. Lucien, tell your men to cover our flanks and to keep their eyes open. I'll guard the king . . . you take the lead."

Lucien hit a fist over his chest before cantering off to relay the orders.

Soon Tarragon found himself gaping in wonder at the canopy above him. He could not see the sky through the thickness of the foliage. His *septurecce* snorted and clicked its tongue beneath him, taking a nervous sidestep. Sensing the unease, the other beasts slowed down to a walk. There was a stillness in the air that made Tarragon's hair stand on its ends. He reached out with his mind, but he sensed nothing other than the minds of smaller animals who looked curiously at them from their hiding places. He sensed more minds, but they were asleep. Most likely hibernating in their dens.

They continued their trek until the trail they followed cut sharply down, angling between jagged outcrops of rocks and scraggly trees growing between them. Soon, it was impossible to go through astride the *septurecce*, so Tarragon called for a halt so they could lead their beasts through the narrow descent. Brenn had to help Tarragon on the more difficult paths. The only good thing was that the path was big enough for the six-legged *septurecce*, who didn't seem to mind when it became more and more difficult to travel.

Chapter Twelve

The sun looked like a white orb in the sky when they finally reached the edge of the forest. Disturbed from the noise and smell of strange animals and men, birds took flight from the trees in a cacophony of cries and crows. Anxious to reach safety and warmth, Tarragon did not think to complain. He wasn't one to grumble, but he was freezing, and he knew the others were, too. They were patient enough. Lucien, though, nothing stopped him from muttering curses loudly. Brenn merely smiled at the other man's discomfort, as though he secretly relished the constant stream of curses and grumbles.

By the time the sun was high, though from the wind chill it seemed a useless orb hanging above them, Tarragon thought his muscles were most likely frozen through. Then a call rose from one of the patrols in the lead. Brenn reached out a hand and pulled Tarragon ahead, hurrying him to the front, where a dozen men stood with swords and bows strapped to their sides and backs. Although their size and uniformity looked menacing, Tarragon sensed nothing but curiosity from them.

"Well come, brothers," the nearest figure spoke in a surprisingly sing-song voice beneath the helmet he wore. "Who is it that you seek?"

Tarragon moved forward to speak, but Brenn laid a steadying hand on his forearm and stepped up.

"We honor your lord and house, brother. I am Brenn, Guardian to the king of the royal house of Dacron. May I know who I am speaking with?"

The one who spoke didn't move, but Tarragon could feel the amusement radiating from him. The man—at least, Tarragon assumed it was a man—was dressed in some sort of attire in shiny black armor that clung closely to his form. The helmet he wore didn't have the metal visor Tarragon was used to. This version had a reflective surface. It looked like glass, but it was a kind that Tarragon had never seen before. From its surface, he saw his reflection look back at him before it moved when the man turned from him back to Brenn.

"I am Force Commander Lawrence, Guardian." Lawrence turned to face Tarragon fully, briefly tilting his head. "You must be the young king Tarragon. How fare you, young sire?"

Tarragon didn't know how to react. He hadn't missed the sarcasm and amusement, nor was he used to that type of behavior around him from people before. As a prince, he'd always been met with some form of respect. Although Lawrence didn't display that respect to his station, Tarragon couldn't find fault, for he sensed no disrespect either. And what was with the old-fashioned speech? Where did that come from? The whole situation was confusing. To hide his uncertainty, he didn't respond immediately.

"You're correct, yes, you are speaking to the new king," Brenn said conversationally. "Now that you know who we are, can we request to speak to your lord?"

Lawrence stared at Brenn for a moment longer before turning to Tarragon once more. "Well come, sire. Our Lord has been expecting you, though we didn't think you'd be here this early. Come, you must be tired and hungry. For your safety, we shall need to proceed to the manor immediately. Also, my men are getting restless—they do not appreciate being this close to the borders."

"Why are they anxious, if you don't mind my asking?"

Tarragon looked at the men standing behind Lawrence. They, too, were wearing the same type of armor, but where Tarragon could see a shadow of a face behind Lawrence's visor, he couldn't see past the matte black of the others. Somehow, Tarragon felt discomfited. He sent a gentle probe into the men's minds, but he drew back almost as soon as he began. It was not that he couldn't see what was in their minds, but it had been like seeing through dirty glass. That surprised him. It hadn't felt natural, either. He could sense their minds, no question. He just knew he would have had to work through that strange barrier.

"You may read into our minds on a later date, sire." Lawrence glanced briefly back at him. "But for now, we must hurry. As I said, our Lord has been expecting you."

"Why are you in such a rush?"

Tarragon looked over his shoulder at Lucien's question. The former bandit was casually leaning on a staff. Where he'd pulled it out from, Tarragon had no idea, for he'd never seen it before. It wasn't some crude tool, either. The shiny surface glinted under the weak remnants of sunlight. Everything, the whole situation, was confusing. Brenn wasn't the lowly soldier turned Guardian that he'd thought him to be, and Lucien wasn't who he thought, either. What did that say about his abilities to read men's minds? When a throat cleared, he turned back to see that Brenn had moved to stand beside him and Lawrence and his men had gone up the trail ahead.

"Brenn, remind me why I shouldn't reprimand you for not telling me everything?"

"Hmm, well sire . . . you're kind of the man who now holds the hearts and minds of your clan. Shouldn't you be the one to know if one of your people is lying or not?"

The heat rose in Tarragon's cheeks. "I'm still quite new at this. I'm still getting used to everything."

"I hate to break it to you, sire, but you need to up your game and learn faster."

"It's not as simple as that, Brenn. I was never trained for this."

"You don't have the luxury of waiting for training. You'll have to depend on your self-discipline and what feels right to you. Now, come. We'd best go and follow those men."

"I don't know why I'm second guessing myself all of a sudden."

"I'm curious about that too. What brought this about? You were doing quite well until now."

Tarragon sighed. "I don't know why. I just feel . . . things are moving too fast."

"I agree, but that never stopped you from making the right decisions before. You took charge as if you were meant to take charge and you went and led us out of the mountains back to safety. *After* we defeated those who ambushed us. Where is that take-charge man?" Brenn cleared a branch from their path.

"Thanks," Tarragon said as he took a step to one side to avoid the branch as it swung. He thought about Brenn's question, trudging along the steep path. "I really don't know what I'm doing, Brenn," he finally confessed. "All I know is that we need more allies."

Brenn didn't respond immediately, but when he did, his voice was so low that only Tarragon could hear him. "Forgive me, but your father ruined your family. However, I trust you and am loyal to you, and I wish you knew more. Do you even know if the Kayels are your ally?"

"I told you before, no. All of my family's memories are lost forever. I have nothing to rely on in terms of collective memories. My father wasn't really keen on keeping records, either. He trusted my brothers would receive the memories."

"He was a man who lacked not only intelligence, but insight. Again, forgive me for my harsh words, sire, but it's the truth. I suggest you find out everything you can. If there's one thing I have learned about you, it's that you know how to wing it. However, even I must admit this one may be just a little more of a challenge."

Tarragon let out a sigh. "I wish you hadn't said that, Brenn." He maneuvered his way around a gnarled trunk of a frozen tree. "Just out of curiosity, do you know anything about the Kayels?"

"In fact, I do, sire."

"Well," Tarragon demanded when Brenn didn't continue. "Get on it. Tell me what you know."

"The Kayels have long been infamous for their secrecy regarding their technological development and their position of armed neutrality. You see four soldiers ahead of us, but you can be certain that there are about fifty that have surrounded us, and that whoever is in charge of their team knows exactly where we are and most likely have trained their weapons on us. They are a technologically advanced society. But because they have been scorned by men like your father, they have chosen not to share anything unless they go through rigid negotiations. Once they're past that, the monetary exchange is usually enough to break even the richest of families. Politically, they are active in pursuing a Kayel-first policy. Meaning, they don't give a shit whether or not the world around them is falling apart. As long as their people are safe, they're neutral. Having said that, they are also active in making sure that peace and order is maintained in and around their borders."

"So what you're saying is, we may not be able to gain them as allies."

"Maybe not as easily, no. Then again, I may be mistaken."

Tarragon didn't have the chance to respond immediately as he had to jump over a narrow watercourse. When he was safely on the ground once more, he looked at the backs of the soldiers ahead of them. They didn't even turn to check whether they were still following, but after what Brenn had just told him, maybe they didn't need to, because whoever was watching them already knew. He shook his head. Something didn't make sense if they were such a closed-minded people.

"What about the mages, Brenn? Do you know anything about that?"

"What I know is what everyone else does, that the lord of that time offered sanctuary to the mages when they were expelled from their homes."

"I can't believe I was not even taught that," Tarragon muttered before letting out a curse. "I hate this. I don't even know when the mages were expelled. They redacted that bit of history from my lessons."

"They were expelled about a millennia ago, sire."

"Guardian, if you have to tell history to the king, can you please make sure to at least pretend to make it a little more complete than what you have just told him?"

Tarragon looked over his shoulder to see that Lucien had once more joined them. The man was using his metal staff to keep himself upright. The ground was uneven, and rushing through to join them must have unbalanced him slightly. When he reached Brenn's side, he slowed down his walk, but he still swayed.

"Eight hundred eighty-five years, young sire. The mages were not expelled. They asked to be expelled. Big difference. They didn't appreciate being used by their kings as pawns for military exercises. When the Kayels opened their borders to welcome them, they upheld the political and military neutrality. And then, they disappeared."

"Did they really disappear, though?" Brenn shot back. "Or did they choose to live a life of peace? Safe from being forced to use their talents by the military?"

Tarragon was intrigued. More and more he was leaning on the belief that Lucien was right about Brenn's background. Was his Guardian really a mage in disguise? And if so, how was it that he was here guarding his back day and night? Despite his worry, Tarragon didn't feel in danger. Brenn was someone he trusted and who made him feel safe. Especially at night, when they lay together in bed. Brenn made him feel not only safe, but sane. He suddenly wished they had more chances to be together. Despite their sleeping together, they hadn't really gone beyond sleeping. Somehow, they never had the chance, and if they did, there were just too many people around. Every single time.

Tarragon closed his eyes. Partly, it was to hide his ever increasing and embarrassing need to do something with Brenn that did not involve his brain or his talent. But also it was to hide his amusement when Lucien started cursing his clumsiness. Tarragon peered under his lashes and quickly stamped on his urge to laugh out loud. Lucien, despite the staff to help him keep his balance, had managed to lose not only it, but also his left boot in the mud.

When Lucien finally got his diminishing dignity back in order, Tarragon and Brenn had stopped walking. The four soldiers had stopped walking as well, and Lawrence was tapping a curious looking apparatus strapped to his forearm. When he was done, Lawrence looked up and waited until they stopped before him. He raised a hand and tapped a finger to the right of his helmet. Immediately, the glass panel slid up to reveal familiar violet eyes.

Tarragon blinked, confused that he should see the color on someone who didn't look at all similar to Brenn. He turned to his Guardian, only to see a broad smile breaking over his face. Lawrence and Brenn met each other halfway and clasped hands. Tarragon's brows rose when Brenn hooked an arm over Lawrence's shoulders and gave him a brief hug.

"Well met, big brother," Lawrence said.

Tarragon's brows went even higher when Brenn kissed the side of Lawrence's face. "Well met, Lawryboy, how is our father?"

"Quite well, Brenn. Missing you. We've all missed you." Lawrence glanced at Tarragon.

"So. This is the young king you've brought us?" Lawrence made a show of examining Tarragon. He ignored Tarragon's startled yelp and turned back to Brenn. "Are you sure he's the one?"

Brenn nodded. He hadn't looked at Tarragon once since that surprising greeting. "I'm not one hundred percent, but yes, I have no doubt it is he we've been waiting for."

"Your sacrifice was well worth it, then. Thank the Goddess." Lawrence turned to Tarragon, and with a toothy smile, gave him the royal salute. His back straight, feet together and a slight bow to his head, he clapped a fist to his chest. "Well come, sire. Please forgive my brother's lies and subterfuge, but all his actions were meant to protect you and our future alliance. The Lord Vale of House Kayel is waiting for you at the manor. Please, I know you're maybe feeling a little angry and have a lot of questions, but we need to take you to the manor as quickly as possible. The border securities are once more in place, but we are out in the open. If you would permit?" Lawrence stepped to one side and waited for Tarragon's response.

"Yes, thank you. I'll permit. Take me to your lord as soon as possible. The trip was a little exhausting, and I must admit that I am tired and hungry. I look forward to a roof over my head. I trust I'm not a prisoner?"

"A prisoner? On the contrary, sire. If Brenn is to be believed, you're the man we've all been waiting for these past eight hundred years. No, you're not a prisoner. You're our savior."

Lawrence grinned even more broadly. With laughter in his voice, he led the way to a vehicle the likes of which Tarragon had never encountered before. It was made entirely out of some metal and hovered about two feet over the ground. It had no wheels. What was this place?

Tarragon kept his thoughts to himself, especially over the admission that his trusted Guardian had lied and kept things from him. Curiously, he was not angry at all. In fact, he felt a relief rush through him. He'd imagined all sorts of difficulties to reach the Kayel lands and search for the mage community, but it seems that was not going to be as difficult as he'd imagined it to be. Best of all, the alliance was about to be served to him without protest.

Tarragon allowed himself to be led and seated inside the vehicle. It was quite luxurious, with leather seats and warm rugs for their legs. On a tray was a glass container which Brenn opened, then pouring its contents into a large cup. Sniffing at the welcoming aroma of meaty soup, Tarragon graciously accepted the cup offered him. His fingers met those of Brenn's, but he made sure not to acknowledge it. When their gazes met, Tarragon held it for a moment before looking away. He heard Brenn sigh and ignored that, too. He might not be mad, he might be on a journey that would be the answer to him ending the war, but Brenn had betrayed him for his failure to tell him everything. His trust for Brenn had splintered, and he didn't know what to think or do about it.

CHAPTER THIRTEEN

The ride to the manor was short enough, though Tarragon didn't know if it was because he was lost in his own thoughts as he planned what to say during the meeting, because the vehicle traveled fast. He'd taken one look outside the side windows and immediately felt dizzy. The scenery rushed by in a blur of colors, and his eyes couldn't keep up. The next time he'd looked out was when they were engulfed in total darkness.

"What's going on? Where are we going?" Tarragon thanked the Goddess that it was Lucien who'd asked the question. He couldn't afford to admit feeling worried.

"We've entered a hillside and are now traveling underground. In a tunnel. It's the fastest and safest way to the manor," Brenn said. He sat opposite Tarragon and had not taken his gaze off him. It really should have made him uncomfortable, but Tarragon had successfully blocked himself off from Brenn's scrutiny. He didn't want the distraction, but he couldn't help glancing every now and then to Brenn's legs in front of him. Brenn's trousers hugged his long limbs, making Tarragon want to rub his hands over them, just to get a feel of those hard thighs. He knew Brenn saw him watching him, but he didn't care. And in any case, he was too busy thinking about the meeting with the Lord.

He couldn't even remember what the man's name was!

The shadows shifted as they went deeper into the tunnel. It felt like it was sloping downward, but Tarragon couldn't really be certain. He looked out and was met with nothing but darkness, and he had to blink once or twice to try to get his eyes adjusted. Inside the vehicle, the noise outside was muffled, which Tarragon was not too comfortable with. As they went deeper, and he guessed lower still, he thought he could see some type of illumination ahead. He studied it as they passed by and saw they were globes of electric lights, much like the ones his father had installed several years after he'd purchased the generators. What made Tarragon curious was he that could not hear any humming sounds he associated with those machines. Also, the lights here were steady whereas he was used to flickering light. He pondered the difference in the results until the only conclusion he reached was that his father had bought something that these people had no use for any longer.

The vehicle banked to the right, and Tarragon thought that instead of descending, he could feel the pull of gravity. More likely they were ascending. It didn't take much time after that, a few seconds really, until Tarragon saw more of the globes lining the tunnel walls. Before his eyes, the light brightened, and he could actually see outside. He saw that the tunnel had widened, and at a short distance, natural light could be seen. The vehicle slowed down, and Tarragon had to blink against the brightness. He knew it was almost evening, so most likely there were more of those electric lights. When he opened his eyes, he stared in surprise at the wonder he beheld.

Before him wound a long driveway lined with flowering trees. Beyond that lay a sprawling estate whose architecture put Tarragon's home to shame. The manor was immense, at least three times the size of Dacron palace. Made of gray and light stone, it was poised upon a mound of earth that gave it an impression of looking over the vast expanse of the territory it lay upon.

When their vehicle finally stopped, it did so at the bottom

of a stairway lined with more of those uniformed soldiers. But for their scarlet capes and silver-hilted swords, they were dressed much like Lawrence and his men. Tarragon jerked in surprise when the door beside him opened. A soldier stood to one side and held the door wide, and Tarragon stepped out. He gazed around him, trying his best to keep his face expressionless. The sight that greeted him was overwhelming. Never had he seen such intricate beauty before.

Standing behind the manor was a mountain, so vast and bluish in the winter light. The cold breeze carried with it unusual scents that one would normally sense only in summer months. He noted the rich smell of flowers and leaves. Frozen fronds of trees raised skyward, and beyond them, wrought by the most skilled of architects, rose the buildings. As if spun by the artisans, spirals rose from domed buildings that glowed faintly in the distance. Streets spanned the gaps between the buildings. Upon them scampered odd vehicles that zipped across. Something hummed in the air, and Tarragon looked up. Up in the air above, a sight he'd never thought possible that made him almost take a step back. Winged vehicles flew. These were not something he'd ever seen before nor heard of, but there they were. One passed lower than the others, and he saw accenting stripes that he recognized as the flag of Oflor.

"Sire, please allow me to take you up to the lord's manor. The sentries you see will accompany us." Lawrence guided their party up the stairs until they reached the landing covered in cobbled stone.

"Allow me to take you directly to the lord, sire." Lawrence didn't wait for Tarragon's response as he hurried them across the way. They finally entered the immense home, and once more, his surroundings amazed Tarragon. He'd never seen such riches before, and he thought he was a king. He doubted if his father even knew what the Kayels were worth.

Lawrence indicated they should wait before he left them in a room that Tarragon thought would be called a sunroom. The entire wall was made entirely out of glass that looked out into a view of gardens draped under the weight of snow. Tarragon looked down and thought he could see some form of maze directly below him. He maintained his composure with effort. He was out of his league, and once more he found himself regretting that he had not been deemed worthy of a better education by his father.

"Are you all right?"

Tarragon took a deep breath and let it out slowly. He moved his hand slightly to the right until he felt Brenn's hand. To his amazement, Brenn moved away, but just as Tarragon felt the first stirrings of regret, his hand was clasped in Brenn's. The next breath he let out unsteadily was one of relief. Gently, tentatively, Tarragon lowered his mental shields and reached out to his Guardian. He almost lost his poise over the emotion he found there. Tarragon opened his mouth, only to look behind him when the doors opened.

The man who was being assisted into the room was quite old. He wore black like the clothing worn by his soldiers, but his were obviously made of soft cloth that was meant to be both elegant and warm. The man had an aura about him that was a blend of dignity, gentility, and surprisingly, a strength of will that was at odds to his frailty. The man turned an amused face to Tarragon as he came nearer.

"Ahh, you are truly a son of the Dacron. You have your mother's eyes, though."

Delighted at the mention of the mother he'd never known, Tarragon moved forward so he could shake the man's hand.

"Lord Kayel, I must presume?"

"Aha! You cannot remember my name. Tsk tsk, that's all right, young man. Yes, I am the Lord Kayel, but you may call me Uncle Vale. Now let me shake that hand."

Taken aback, Tarragon shook the Lord's hand. At once, he felt the thin skin, and a rush of welcome emanated from the man. "Uncle? Oh, of course, out of respect, of course, I can call you uncle." Tarragon licked his lips nervously. Why was it that he felt like a child next to this man?

"No, not out of respect, although that would most certainly help. I am really your uncle, nephew. Well . . ." Lord Vale stopped and pursed his lips in thought. He muttered something inaudible, then grinned. "I had to think there, but I figured out that you are my nephew sixteen times removed. Now, sit me down. I'm feeling my age, and I'm not as young as you are."

Tarragon found himself helping the lord to a plush seat. When he was seated, one of his assistants draped a blanket over his knees. The lord waved the man away with a click of his tongue. He glared at the man when he was ignored in favor of laying a shawl over his shoulders. When he was done, the servant stood behind the lord's chair and stared into space.

"Forgive my manservant, nephew. He fusses most of the time, and he is not liking it that I decided to meet you here instead of in my chambers."

"Oh, I . . . do I need to apologize?" Tarragon felt ridiculous. He didn't know how to act. And he was supposed to be a king and the old man a mere lord?

"Nonsense, nephew. Of course not. You're king!" The lord made a sound that suggested amusement. "I see the Kayel in your eyes, nephew, but I also sense a talent only the mages here display. Tell me, has my son taught you how to control your talent?"

"Uhm . . . I don't know your son, sir. But yes, I'm slowly

beginning to have better control of it, though I still don't understand how it works."

"Brenn! What have you been doing this past year? Didn't I give specific instructions for you to teach this young man the tricks of the trade?"

"I apologize, Father. But the former king assigned me somewhere else, and I only got the chance to join King Tarragon a few months ago. And then there was that ambush we had to get through and a whole other . . ." Brenn's voice drifted off when Lord Vale stared intently at him.

Tarragon's mouth dropped open. He looked from one man to the other before finally settling on Brenn. He thought he knew the man. Obviously, he had been ignorant and naïve, thinking . . . he didn't know what to think.

"Excuses. All of it." Lord Vale continued to stare at Brenn. When he looked over at him, Tarragon thought Brenn would wilt under the old man's glare.

Lawrence coughed into his hand, breaking the standoff. "Father, my lord. You're confusing the king. May I suggest you question Brenn later?"

"Humph." Vale sent Brenn one last evil look before turning to face Tarragon once more. "Forgive me, sire. You didn't need to see that family drama. We mages love drama, while your kind love the lack of it. Now, I distract myself. Let's talk about how we're going to form our alliance."

Tarragon's heart pumped wildly before settling. This day was full of too many surprises, and now the added bonus of his dreamed-of alliance was being served on a platter.

"I did come here to seek an alliance with your house, Lord . . . uhm . . . Uncle Vale, but first, why did you say that you were mages?"

"Why, nephew, didn't you know? We, the Kayels, we're all mages by blood."

Tarragon frowned, still confused. "I don't understand.

Brenn told me that the Kayels offered sanctuary to the mages when they were expelled. I thought . . . I don't understand."

"Ah, let me make it simpler, then. When the mages were expelled over eight hundred years ago, they came into our lands, and we accepted them as one of us for as long as they held on to our beliefs and practices. Peace and impartiality was our main thought at that time."

"Are you saying that's all been changed?"

"Not everything is changed, but a huge part of it. Eight hundred years is a long time living together as one clan, sire. It would be illogical to think that our people did not marry each other, because they did. We did. Now all the people of Kayel are mages by birth. But we're also the same Kayels who love to learn and experiment. The only difference between then and now is that we merged our technology and magic together."

"So. What you're saying is that all these technologies, your experiments, and inventions, they are all made through science and magic. But that's impossible."

"Dear nephew, nothing is impossible. We Kayels believe that when there is a will, there is a way. And believe me, nephew. After eight hundred years, we have had the forceful will to guarantee that we will always find a way."

"And your will is?"

When Vale did not answer at once, Tarragon felt a stirring in the air. It was as though everyone around him was holding their breaths. He reached out with his mind and felt a nervousness among the soldiers while Brenn was more stoic, as though he knew what his father was going to say next.

"I would wish for a negotiation," Vale said.

Tarragon felt a stab of concern. Knowing so little about the mages and the Kayels placed him at a disadvantage. The finality of his dream was suddenly too much for him. As his thoughts were racing, he strove to buy some time.

"I haven't rested since we first set out to travel here, Uncle. Perhaps if you could give me a day or two before we start our negotiations?

Lord Vale raised a hand, and immediately his manservant leaned in to listen to his request. When the man left, Vale looked at Tarragon.

"I sent my man to find out about some refreshments. In the meantime, let us begin with the terms for our alliance."

Tarragon took a deep breath before letting it out slowly. If he left now, he might end up offending Lord Vale and lose any chance for an alliance. Suddenly, Tarragon felt every tight muscle in his body. The excitement of reaching Oflor had driven him for days, but now, he felt like collapsing. He started when Brenn stepped forward and bowed his head.

CHAPTER FOURTEEN

"Speak, Brenn," Lord Vale said.

"I fear the king is speaking the truth. He has not rested in his hurry to come here."

"I see," Vale said, turning to Tarragon once more. "I'm curious, nephew. Your talent, tell me about it."

"I'm not sure where to begin," Tarragon said, glancing from Brenn to Vale. "What do you want to know?"

"Tell me about how you feel when the power begins to present itself."

"Well, it's hard to explain, but I feel the power come to me when I'm out in the open, or just recently, I discovered that I felt the generators my father bought from you call to me."

"How different are the two?"

"Well, when I'm around the generators, I begin to feel . . . charged, I guess, is the only way to explain. And when I'm out in the open, I feel the energies in the sky."

"What is it about the sky really? Do you know?"

"Not a call, not like the generator, more like something in the sky pulls me."

"And how do you know when the power is within you?"

"I see this light, sometimes blue, sometimes white. When I'm outside, it's like I can harness the energies from the sky and when I release it, it comes out as white energy. From the generators, it's stronger, and when I harness its energies, they're blue. That energy is somehow stronger, and I feel like I can do almost anything I want or think of doing. I also noticed that it healed me physically. I had a wound on my leg, and I thought I would lose it. But when I harnessed the energy from the generator, my leg healed."

Vale's scrutiny made Tarragon uneasy. The old man's eyes were clouded with age, but it was not difficult to see that they were just as violet as those of the rest of the men he'd met here. So like Brenn's, and yet so different. None of them had the intensity in Brenn's eyes, especially when they were gazing at him. Momentarily distracted, Tarragon hadn't realized that he had been staring at Brenn until Lord Vale began to chuckle.

"Ahh, youthful romance. How I miss those days." Vale patted Tarragon's knee, making him blush at the implication no one was likely to miss.

"Tell me, nephew, what do you wish to have should Oflor become your ally?"

Tarragon sighed. Here was the moment he had been rehearsing for the last week of travel, and now that he was finally face to face with the situation, he didn't know what to say. Just then another black-uniformed soldier came in and whispered something into Lawrence's ear. They exchanged briefly before Lawrence gave a nod and dismissed the messenger.

Lawrence then went over to lean down in his father's ear and said something in a low voice. Although Lord Vale's face didn't change expression, the corners of his eyes tightened. He nodded and waved Lawrence away.

"You'd best hurry with what you want to say to me, young king. Word has it that Caprici troops are but five days from our borders."

Alarm, disappointment, and anger welled up within Tarragon, but alarm prevailed over all other emotions. Somehow, someone had betrayed him. He looked up to meet Lucien's eyes and saw the man had reached the same conclusion.

"May I be excused, sire? I need to see to our men." Lucien's voice was tight, and Tarragon could see that he was going to deal severely with whoever had betrayed them. It didn't matter if the one who did was a Dacron or one of Lucien's.

"I need to know if they were able to breach Dacron's walls, Lucien. I'm sorry for having to send you back, but I can't spare Brenn right now."

"I'll go with my most trusted men, sire. And don't worry about your Guardian, you need him here. I can handle things back home."

"I know you can, Lucien. It's why you're going and not Brenn."

Lucien smirked and saluted him before turning to leave the room.

"Before you go, let me offer some assistance." Lord Vale raised a hand, and immediately Lawrence leaned down once more. Lucien waited where he stood. "Send a few of our men to accompany him. Make sure his journey is swift. Assist him in every way possible."

"Yes, sir. I'll see to it myself," Lawrence said before turning to Lucien. "Shall we?"

The two men left the room. When the door shut behind them, Tarragon faced Lord Vale.

Tarragon did not envy what Lucien had to face on his return across hostile territory, especially with the Caprici troops barring their journey back. Even more disturbing was that the Caprici king knew Tarragon was in Oflor and what the Caprici king knew, the Zaruthra king knew as well. Those two were no mere allies, as they were lovers and shared the same lust for killing every Dracon blooded mortal they could lay their hands on.

"Thank you, Uncle. We need all the help you can give us.

Most of those left at home are either too ill or injured to survive the travel. There are so few of us left."

"Let me educate you about your family, nephew. Did you know that the Dacrons were originally a part of the house of Kayel? When one of their sons married into royalty, they splintered from us to join that clan. However, they never forgot where they came from or what they were. In secret, they made sure to marry into the Kayel family, to ensure the mage line survived. That is the reason why you inherited the gift of a collective memory. However, that was purely a Dacron gift, and you're the only one who has it still. Once the Zaruthra and the Caprici families got wind of the activity a few hundred years back, they thought to bring back their military might by ensuring mage blood ran in theirs, too. That activity was stopped before they could actually succeed but not before they took one of our daughters of the House and killing her in the process. So, my young king, we are not closing any business deals or for military purposes. You will be negotiating about rejoining our family. Our clan. Now speak, nephew. Are you going to come back to Oflor or not?"

Speechless at the revelation about his family's origins, Tarragon sat staring at the lord of Oflor, unable to formulate the words that should save him from looking stupid. Why had he not known this? In hindsight, he didn't think his brothers did, either. Neither had his father. When had that information been expunged from his family's records? Through his dismay, Tarragon saw an advantage. The Kayels were linked by blood with him, the last of the Dacrons. He might use that link for his own gain and guarantee the survival of his clan.

"Brenn." Tarragon motioned for Brenn to come closer. "Please take those who came with us to wait outside. Impress on them that they are not to be permitted to reveal whatever they must have heard." Brenn's gaze locked on his, and Tarragon dropped his mental shields. Should word get out that he was negotiating an alliance with the Kayels and the mages, it could only come from one of the men who had accompanied him there. That included the Kayels as well. Although Brenn did not react too visibly, there was no disguising the tightening on the sides of his mouth. Tarragon had just pronounced the death sentence on any one of the men with them inside the room that might have betrayed them. Brenn nodded once and straightened, his face set in a grim mask.

Tarragon straightened. To Lord Vale, he said, "Shall we proceed?"

CHAPTER FIFTEEN

When the door to his assigned bedroom closed behind him, Tarragon's shoulders sagged in relief. He didn't know whether to laugh out loud or cry. The seeds he'd just sown would change his clan's future, but he knew it would be for the better. At least he hoped so. But for all the successes of the past few days, the shadow of the imminent arrival of the Caprici forces cast a deadly doom over all of them. The clan was known for their military might and absence of moral compass. Their king and military leaders were not known for their compassion. It was no accident or coincidence they were on their way to Oflor. Someone in Tarragon's retinue or one of the servants he'd left behind at home had betrayed him. Who else was there to blame? Of course, he could concentrate and find out for himself, but that would have to wait until he'd rested. Pushing himself would only muddle his brain.

He'd overreached his energies, fatigue overwhelming his thoughts—he'd reached his breaking point, and he knew it. Slowly, with trembling fingers, he started taking off his clothes. Finally free of all clothing, wanting a hot bath badly, he stood at the center of the room looking around, trying to find the bathing room. If he were not so tired, he would have examined each and every unfamiliar piece of furniture and bits of technology that he found everywhere he looked.

The room was luxurious enough. From the heavy material draping the floor-to-ceiling window to the lamps on either side of the magnificently laid out bed, everything screamed opulence and revolutionary technology. There was no doubt in his mind that should the Zaruthrans or Capricis get their way, nothing would hold them back from weaponizing Kayel technology, and he couldn't allow that to happen.

He finally spotted a door off to one side and walked over to it. Hopefully, it would be the bathing room he was seeking.

"Thank the Goddess for small pleasures," he muttered when his assumption proved correct. Whoever had been in charge of his rooms had also made sure to run a bath.

Tarragon sagged into the water and closed his eyes. He brooded under the mist that rose around him—from his actions since the death of his brothers and father, to the decisions he'd made regarding Brenn's promotion to Guardian status, the most trusted position any soldier could accomplish. And then there was Lucien, not quite the Guardian, but a commander nevertheless. The last two decisions posed him the greatest risks of all.

As his aches and pains fell into the heat of the water, Tarragon was content to lie back and doze. In his mind's eye, he watched the many ways his actions would turn out. One by one, his mind went over each, rejecting many, considering others. He was still lost in thought when he heard the unmistakable sound of footsteps. Alarmed, Tarragon sat up only to see that it was Brenn who stood at the doorway.

"You're here," he said, slumping back into the water and closing his eyes. He didn't want Brenn to see the difficulty he was having in keeping his emotions.

"I see you're still upset with me," Brenn said.

"You think?"

Brenn's low chuckle made Tarragon open his eyes once more. He watched as Brenn approach, picked up a stool by the side of the door, set it down by Tarragon's feet and sat on it.

"I apologize for keeping my true identity from you."

"Are you keeping anything else from me?"

"No. That time has passed. You can ask me anything, and I won't hesitate to tell you the truth."

"I'm reconsidering your position, so before I strip you of your rank, can you tell me why you went out of your way to betray me? Or were you grooming me for your . . . nefarious intentions?"

Brenn's response was a brief widening of his eyes before he let out a full out laugh. Tarragon glared at his Guardian, wanting to get out of the water so he could strangle him, but he would be naked. Also, he really didn't want to strangle the man. When Brenn's laughter finally died down, he bit his upper lip and leaned his elbows on his knees.

"I wasn't grooming you. In fact, I was quite surprised when you promoted me on the field that day. Truth is, I was just doing what the others have been doing for the past eight hundred years. There has always been a Kayel who becomes Guardian to a Dacronian prince or princess. It was my turn, and I was assigned to you."

"Are you saying that all this time, my family has been manipulated by the Kayels? By the mages?"

"Yes and no," Brenn said, straightening. He crossed one leg over the other and studied Tarragon. "It has been my family's custom to guide a Dacron should they display any signs of magic. Not the collective memory part, that is exclusive to your family's talent for some reason we could never discover. What I'm talking about is mage talent. When I was first assigned to you, we were already aware that you had a talent. It was only when I finally joined you at that mountain pass that I saw that the talent was more than I'd ever encountered before. You are quite powerful, sire."

"Are you a mage? Do you have any talent?"

"I am a mage, yes. And yes, I have a lot of talent. I'm

Master of the Mages."

"A master?"

"Not a, *the* Master."

"I don't understand. Is that some sort of rank?"

"It is. A Master is someone who has ... mastered the magical arts to a certain degree. In my case, I have mastered most of them."

"I'm thinking that makes you pretty old to have accomplished all that."

"I am."

Tarragon scoffed. "What? Are you telling me that you're a hundred years old or something? An immortal?"

"Well, not that old. And no, I'm not immortal," Brenn said with a huff. The corner of his mouth lifted in a wry grin. "I'm eighty years old."

Tarragon slipped under the water, and it took him a moment to sputter his way to the surface. Was Brenn lying again? The first time he saw him, he thought Brenn looked about his age, but his opinion had changed once he got to know him better. But eighty? Finally resurfacing, he spat out the water that had managed to enter his mouth. In front of him, Brenn hadn't even attempted to help him. The man sat there grinning in amusement. It felt quite embarrassing.

"How is that even possible?" Tarragon cleared the soapy water from his stinging eyes.

"You saw for yourself when you used your talent. The energies you harnessed healed whatever wounds you had at that time. I haven't seen any scarring, either."

"You mean that every time I use my talent, I increase my age? What?"

"No. Your body gets healed every single time. It's one of those life-saving side-effects. It simply increases your chances of maintaining your hold on life as your magic heals your body every time you use it. The more you use your magic, the more chances you have of living longer."

"I take it that you've used your talent a lot?"

"Quite." Brenn grinned.

"Why were you assigned to me? Why not someone else?"

"Because the one previously assigned to you could not handle the kind of talent you displayed. You needed someone of my caliber, so he sought my help."

Tarragon considered who it was that had guarded him. "It was Malcolm, wasn't it?"

"Yes. Your former guardian did everything he could to keep you alive."

"Do you think my father knew?"

Brenn scoffed. "Your father's only saving graces were his begetting you and your brothers and the hereditary collective memory. Other than that, he didn't know what to do with a cut on his finger, even if he had to think about it for a hundred years."

"You really liked him, didn't you?"

"He was a bastard through and through. A disgrace to the bloodline. Then again, I guess we can forgive him for his idiocies. There's always one or two in every generation . . . such is the nature of life."

Tarragon studied his crinkling fingertips. The water was cooling around him, but he didn't stand up.

"Am I still in trouble?"

"When you held me in your arms that first night, was it because you wanted to help me get over my grief, or was it something else altogether?"

The question hung heavily in the air like mist in a forest. When Brenn didn't reply at once, Tarragon's heart clenched painfully even as he fisted his hands under the water. He looked up and saw the open uncertainty on Brenn's face. The emotions warred across it, his violet eyes turning almost a deep purple. His skin paled and flushed in a kaleidoscope of indecision.

The water splashed around Tarragon as he rose from the tub, some of it overflowing to the floor. Brenn didn't move even when his trousers turned dark from soaking up the liquid. Stepping out of the tub, he locked his focus on Brenn's still form, took up a towel warming on a rack, and wrapped it around his waist. Without looking back, he walked out of the bathing room and into the bedroom. He didn't know what to think of Brenn's silence. What he did know was that he needed to hear the answer to his question. His heart depended on it.

CHAPTER SIXTEEN

"I'm eighty years old, Tarragon. Did you not even hear me?" Brenn challenged in a soft voice.

"Just answer the question, Brenn." Tarragon stood in front of an open wardrobe, searching for something to wear. He had seen it earlier and now looked inside. Clothing hung to one side, while on the shelves were more items, folded and arranged neatly on a stack. Taking a pair of trousers, Tarragon began to put them on. "Did you do it to help your king, or was it for some other reason? Did you do it knowing that I've always found you attractive since I first saw you that day in the pass?"

"What would people say? I'm technically only your Guardian, a cousin several times removed. You're a king. You are destined for something else."

"What are they going to say? That you're a man? No one would care. That you're old enough to be my great grandfather? They will only make a fuss if they find out your actual age. Tell me something else."

"I'm not destined to be your consort, Tarr. Someone else is."

"Who? Who am I destined for? Someone I will not have any feelings for? Someone who will most likely be a woman who will bear my children?"

Brenn shrugged. "Not necessarily. My parents didn't need a woman to have their sons. As they produced six sons between them, I don't see that as a problem. That issue's been dealt with by my people over a hundred years now."

Unable to comprehend what Brenn was talking about, Tarragon could only stare at him. Then he shook his head and continued putting on his clothes.

"I'm only king because of you, Brenn. Don't you know that? Haven't you realized it? It was because of you that I haven't gone insane from grief and indecision and . . . and fear. Do you know how scared I was, Brenn? That day at home, when I saw, when we discovered my family's bodies? Do you know what that did to me?" Tarragon's voice broke, and to his shame, tears welled in his eyes. His face crumpled, and his mouth trembled. He sniffled before furiously wiping at his eyes, and then he pulled out a shirt from its hanger. Even to his own ears, his breaths sounded muffled and raspy. Surely Brenn could see that he was holding on to his pride. But who cared, when Tarragon knew he could never hide his true self from his Guardian.

"How can you stand there and ask those questions when you know what I went through? You were the only one I didn't hide from, Brenn. You . . . you . . . Goddess, without you, I would have died. Don't you realize that?" More tears fell, and he let out a low scream of frustration when his trembling fingers refused to move as they should. Why were the buttons not cooperating? Tarragon sniffed back the tears and tried the button again, but he failed. "No . . . please, just get in the damned hole, please."

And then Brenn was there, his warm hands taking hold of Tarragon's trembling ones and stilling them. Slowly, gently, one by one, he pried them away from the offending buttons and took over the task. Tarragon's shoulders stiffened, but he didn't say anything. He bit on his lower lip, wiping away the tears when they continued to fall, watching Brenn finish buttoning his shirt.

"I lost my childhood a long time ago, Brenn. Didn't Malcolm tell you? About how my father made sure I never had a

111

childhood? It was Malcolm who taught me how to read and write, to wield a sword, to experiment on my talent, only at that time I didn't know that what he was teaching me to control and wield was mage talent. It was he who made sure my brothers treated me equally, too. I don't know how he did it, but he convinced my brothers' Guardians to make sure I got treated well."

"Like me and Malcolm, they were sent there to be your Guardians, Tarr," Brenn said, his voice soft and soothing. Tarragon started to calm down, his heart slowing down to a steadier beat.

"Were they from Oflor, too? My brothers' Guardians?"

"Yes. As I told you earlier, all royal Dacrons are guarded by the Kayels."

"Did you know them? Were they your friends?"

"Yes, we grew up together. One of them was my younger brother. Steven. He was your brother Konrad's Guardian." Brenn looked up and met Tarragon's gaze. "You see, I, too, am grieving, Tarr. Steven was no mage like me, but he was a great soldier, and he taught your brother the ax."

"I liked Steven, but he didn't look like you. Well, not really, and he didn't have your violet eyes."

"As I said, he was not a mage, and he took after my father."

"I know your father is Vale." Tarragon frowned. Was there more to Brenn's secrets?

"I have two fathers. My other father, Dennis, *he* was the mage. He was much older than my father, Vale, and we lost him over twenty years ago. To old age."

"How can that be? Did you have a surrogate mother? What were you telling me earlier?"

Brenn grinned as he took out a coat and helped Tarragon into it. "Not us, no. Others do have surrogates, but both of my fathers decided they wanted their children to come from both of them."

"Pretend I'm an idiot and explain to me how two men can have children, will you?"

This time, Brenn laughed. "Well, after dinner, I can take you to the viewing room so I can show you, tell you, all about Oflor's secrets. We're very advanced and have made sure that no one on the outside knows just how."

"What has that got to do with two men having children?"

"Technology, remember? Come on, let's have something to eat, not keep my father waiting. I know you're tired, but you need to hold on a while longer."

"You still didn't answer my question, Brenn." He searched into Brenn's eyes, hoping to see the answers there.

Brenn shook his head. "You've always been hard-headed," he said. He moved closer, and Tarragon's breath hitched in his throat.

When Brenn's mouth settled on his, Tarragon stilled before yielding under the pressure. He opened his mouth slightly, just enough to allow Brenn's breath to mingle with his. The taste of those lips on his overwhelmed him. He'd kissed men before, but it was always different with Brenn.

Tarragon didn't complain when Brenn captured his face with his hands. The heated skin felt coarse and calloused. Brenn tilted Tarragon's head up and leaned down to claim his mouth in a hard and undeniable kiss filled with lust and need. Tarragon felt the energy exchange between them, felt his energy crawl from under his skin until it met that coming from Brenn. Funny how he'd not realized before that every time they kissed and the heat flared between them, it had been their energies reaching out to each other, merging as one and enveloping them both. Just as he realized this, the heat got hotter, making Tarragon tremble.

The crawling, twisting energies came from the depths of his stomach up through his chest, and suddenly, it was almost unbearable. He really should be in pain, but he wasn't. Instead, he felt like he was being cradled in a sea of flame, stealing the air from his lungs, swallowing him deep, almost like drowning. He opened his mouth under Brenn's assault, their breaths mingling and suddenly, he wasn't drowning.

Brenn took command of his lips, much like he'd taken command of Tarragon's life, but instead of pulling him headlong someplace where he didn't want to be, Brenn knew exactly how to cajole a response from Tarragon, luring him into a place he didn't want to leave.

Gasping for breath, Tarragon tore his mouth from under Brenn's. At the same time, he clutched at the arms that held him, searching, needing the strength that lay concealed beneath the uniform.

"We're going to be late for dinner," Tarragon said, his breath sounding wobbly.

"Then I guess we get ourselves together, why don't we?"

For a moment, Tarragon couldn't stop the need that rushed up from his groin, and with nothing else to do, he arched up against Brenn. He'd had flings before, but they had been with boys his own age, princes and lordlings who didn't know much more than he. Before Brenn, he'd never been kissed by someone who knew what to do and made him feel more than he'd ever felt before. He raised his head and met those lips once more, pressing closer until his and Brenn's groins and chests flattened against one another.

Brenn tasted of all things lust and need, and something more. Tentatively, still remembering the mental slap he'd received earlier for daring to intrude on Brenn's mind, Tarragon sent a mental touch. He smiled into Brenn's mouth when he felt the mental caress, and his blood felt heavier and hotter and sweeter. The kiss continues until he felt his body grow so tight that when he dared take a breath, the pull on his groin made his cock ache.

This was what Tarragon needed. Temptation in the form of Brenn's body, his kiss, his taste, this was what he wanted more than food. But then a gong sounded loudly from somewhere, startling Tarragon from Brenn's arms. He looked about wildly for the source of the sound when Brenn's chuckle made him turn to Brenn once more.

"We're being summoned," Brenn said as he ran a trembling hand through his hair. "We have to go."

"Are we being monitored here?" Tarragon looked about once more, trying to see if there were something that would make him uncomfortable.

"No, at least, not in this room. However, we're late going down, and Father doesn't care for a cold meal." Brenn held out his hand toward the door.

Tarragon thought about making up an excuse so he and Brenn could stay in the room for the night, but then his stomach's startling disagreement by gurgling loudly took matters out of his hands.

"Dinner it is."

Chapter Seventeen

Tarragon found himself enjoying his dinner. He had thought that he was too exhausted to eat anything, but when the simple broth was served and he took his first mouthful, he found his appetite returning and didn't put down the spoon until he'd emptied his bowl. When his bowl was replaced with a dish of meat and vegetables, he took up his knife and attacked it wordlessly. He'd gotten used to eating military rations, and even the food served in Dacron Palace had been unappetizing. This feast laid out before him was something like what he'd taken for granted while growing up. No thanks to the war, good food had gone scarce.

"I see you've regained your appetite, nephew."

Tarragon snapped back to the present, disoriented for a moment before he remembered to chew more slowly before taking up the wine cup and taking a swallow.

"I apologize, I haven't eaten this well for almost two years, Uncle."

Lord Vale gave him an indulgent smile. "There's more where that's coming from. I've been to war myself. I can still remember that first time I ate a proper meal after a long while. No need to apologize."

A servant came in and hurried over to where Vale sat at the head of the table. Tarragon couldn't hear what the man was saying into Vale's ear, but when the old man's face paled, Tarragon had a sudden sense of déjà vu. His heart thudded in raw fear. Vale said something to the servant, who straightened and left the room, shutting the door behind in a soft click. Vale turned to Tarragon, taking the cloth napkin from his lap and laying it on the table.

"Sire, I've just received some interesting news." Vale stood up as he spoke.

"Trouble?" Tarragon surmised.

Vale returned with a curt nod. "Lawrence has sent word from Dacron Palace."

Tarragon didn't have time to wonder at the speed with which Lawrence and Lucien had crossed the miles back to Dacron. They had only been gone several hours. He slumped into his chair, feeling a sudden crush to the hope he'd felt at his accomplishment earlier in the day. Looking at Vale, he saw that the man was gifted in breaking news cleanly.

"What did he say?"

"The place is surrounded by Caprici forces. They're two or three days out yet, but your man Lucien is asking permission to transport your men over here."

Distracted by horrible images of what would happen to the rest of his people, Tarragon had to force himself back to track on the immediate issue.

"How would that be possible? We're talking about two or three hundred people, not to mention the rest of Lucien's people. Before we came out here, he'd sent out his son to gather them and bring them over to my home. Not to mention we'd have to leave our *septurecce*." Tarragon didn't speak about the loss of those beasts. The Capricis had coveted them for years. Even if his father had been incompetent as a king, there was one thing he had been very good at. The *septurecce* in their pens had been bred brilliantly, and their worth was more than their weight or their strength. Their beasts were highly intelligent and loyal, something that the others had never managed to breed properly.

"Father, may I have your permission to take the Menace?

We're the fastest and best equipped. We'll be there and back by tomorrow at sunset if we leave now."

Tarragon whirled in surprise at Brenn's offer.

"What's the Menace?"

"He's talking about his squadron, the Master Mage's Menaces."

"A squadron." Tarragon blinked. "You have a squadron?"

Brenn flashed him a brief grin. "I do." Looking at his father once more, he continued. "Father?"

"That's not all that Lawrence said," Vale said in a worried tone. "One of his scouts saw siege engines hidden within their ranks. They said they were disguised as food wagons, but logic told him otherwise."

"What gave them away?" Brenn took a step forward with his head tilted to one side.

"Their weight. The wheels were too wide and large for regular wagons, and they dug deep into the ground."

"It's winter. The ground's solid," Tarragon said.

Vale nodded at Tarragon. "Exactly. It would be logical to assume that the Capricis share equipment with the Zaruthrans, which means you and Lawrence have to be back here as fast as you could. We can defend Oflor, but we'll need all hands here." Vale turned to Tarragon. "How precious are those beasts of yours?"

"Very, but if they need to be sacrificed, so be it."

"You would never be able to replicate your father's work on them," Brenn said, looking grim.

"I would rather save my people than the beasts, but no, I wouldn't be able to replicate anything. His memories are lost to me so all we'll be able to save of their breed would be the beasts themselves."

"Brenn, go and get those men and women out, but tell them they cannot take anything with them. Tell them there's no more room. If you can, get all those beasts into whatever space is leftover. However, I think you need to talk to Tarragon here before you do." He turned to leave. "Make it fast, son. Your very life depends on it."

"I want to go with you," Tarragon said before the door closed behind Vale.

As he expected, Brenn immediately shook his head. "No. I'd be too distracted to keep you safe. You need to stay here. I'll assign the best guardsmen to stay with you. I'll be back tomorrow afternoon."

Tarragon gritted his teeth and stood his ground. He'd die first if he were to stay in Oflor. "No. I insist on going with you. Those are my people out there, Brenn. And you know I can fight just as well as any guardsmen. Plus, I have my talent. You can't stop me."

"I can if I need to."

Tarragon stared at his Guardian, reaching out with his mind to try to see just how stubborn he was going to be about this. Immediately, a mental slap like he'd never encountered before hit him like a physical blow, making him wince and take a step back. He held a hand to his head as he looked on at Brenn in surprise.

"Don't you ever do that again," Brenn said, biting the words out. His eyes glowed bright, the flashes across them making Tarragon see for the first time the strength in his magic. "It is not only ungentlemanly, it is downright intrusive, and frankly, a violation of my mental space. Have I been mistaken in thinking that you are different from your father?"

"Excuse me? I've been inside your mind before. Why are you suddenly so defensive? What exactly are you hiding from me? Earlier you said you were never going to lie to me again, and it's not even two hours yet, and you already are!"

"First of all," Brenn said as he took a step forward,

"before when you were in my mind, you were acting as my king and making sure your people were not going insane from the loss of the connection. Second, I am not lying to you. I told you we were going to talk about everything tonight, but given as we haven't even finished eating dinner, I haven't had the chance."

Tarragon pressed his lips tight. He knew he was being stupidly obstinate, but at that moment, he really didn't care. He had to make Brenn agree, but he didn't know how. "All right, I'll give you that, but I am still going with you, and that's final."

"You are not, and my men will listen to me. I am their commander."

"Yes, but I am their king. Already I feel their minds and have touched a few of them. They are as much a part of my people as my clan are."

"True, but they don't know you. They will not listen to you."

"I can make them!" As soon as the words burst out of his mouth, he knew he'd made a mistake and regretted it instantly.

Brenn's face darkened, and before Tarragon could retract his careless words, Brenn's face was in his so fast that he had to take a nervous step backward. It was not as much from fear but from trying to get out of the way of Brenn's anger.

"How dare you think to presume that because your inheritance has gifted you with the talent to help your people you have the right to abuse their wills!"

"Brenn, I have to be there!" Tarragon knew he'd crossed the line, and shame swept over him, but he had to make Brenn understand. "We've already lost everything else, how can I not be with them when I could lose them all? I won't give my people up without a fight. If the Dacron line ends with me, so be it, but I refuse to have my faithful men left in disfavor with the Goddess. If they lose their lives defending an absent king, then I will end my life myself." His voice shook as he gazed into Brenn's disappointment.

Ever since his brothers' deaths, it seemed like his life was a series of calamitous events that couldn't wait to trample his life even more as fast as possible. Was the Goddess so cruel as to thrust him into this situation so young in life, ill-prepared to rule, just as he had the means to save his people within arm's reach? If only he knew how and where to begin—to have a ready-made plan he could use against the advantages his enemies seemed to have in overabundance. Goddess, he had the technology and the talents of the mages served him on a platter and yet he still felt impotent to the cruelty of those who coveted his family's name.

"Tarr, we haven't lost yet," Brenn prompted gently.

Tarragon almost sagged in relief, unable to stand against Brenn's anger. Had he come to rely on the man too much? Overly so? What did that say about his kingly status?

"Tarr?"

Tarragon repressed his fears with a violent tremor he refused to control. "I agree, I shouldn't have said what I said, and that will be the last time I or any of my line will utter those words. Should I live, you and your father have full permission to guarantee my descendants will never make the same mistake. I don't care how you do it. But I need to be in Dacron, and I know you can stop me. But you won't. Not because you can't, but because Goddess knows once you do so, I won't be able to resist your will. I love you too much to defy you." He stepped closer until only a breath separated them. "I also know you love me, and you respect me enough to realize that I am not only Tarragon standing here in front of you, but your king. I am the Dacron king, and my people will only fight when I am there for them to see and to spur them on. They may have lost a lot, but they are a mighty force once they see they have the advantage of your armies and your technology." Tarragon leaned forward and pressed his forehead against Brenn's. "Please, Brenn."

The seconds ticked passed, slower than he could ever imagine, and still, Brenn didn't speak. He didn't move away, either. By that, Tarragon was assured Brenn was thinking over what he said. Finally, Brenn let out a huff, his breath smelling a mixture of the food he'd just eaten and the alcohol he'd drunk. They mingled with Brenn's unique scent, and briefly Tarragon lost himself in the moment, wishing their situation wasn't so dire. Brenn stepped away and snapped him a salute.

"Your will, my king."

Tarragon took in a tremulous breath. "Go and get your squadron ready. Once you have everything taken care of, come for me. No, better yet, do you have anyone who can get to me fast?"

"Even better." Grinning, Brenn took something from his belt and handed it to Tarragon. "Here. We use this to communicate with each other. Press the blue button when you want to say something. Release it to listen for the reply."

Tarragon eagerly reached for the small black mechanism. It didn't look or feel as though it weighed anything. "A messaging device?" He raised his gaze up to Brenn's amused ones. "You have a messaging device. This is extraordinary."

"If you're excited about that little thing, wait until you get on the Justice."

Tarragon looked up to see Brenn's face breaking into an excited grin. "You look as if you're about to burst with pride, Guardian. What is this Justice?"

"It's my flyer. We can take off and land on a spot, and its equipped with everything one needs to communicate with others in real time."

"Does it have weapons?"

"Yes. All the flyers have them. We'll make fast work of getting our people out."

"And my herd of *septurecce*?"

"No promises, but yes, them too. I know how important they are to you."

"Thank you, Brenn."

"Go and get ready. We leave in an hour." Brenn turned around to leave the room.

"Where do I meet you?"

Brenn paused at the question and had a faraway look in his eyes as he thought it over. "I'm not sure, but I'll let you know. If I don't get you myself, I'll send someone over to take you." Without waiting for Tarragon's reply, he strode toward the doors, leaving Tarragon to gaze at his retreating back. He looked around him until his focus settled on the table, the food on their plates unfinished. For a moment, he warred against going back to his room or sitting back down. It was his stomach that made the decision for him, so he sat back down and took up his knife and fork. The meat was cold, but it still tasted good, and he hurried to finish. It wasn't good to waste food when he didn't know when his next meal was going to be.

CHAPTER EIGHTEEN

The journey back to Dacron had only taken them an hour at most, and he'd reveled at the speed of which they'd traveled. The brief disappointment he'd felt when he'd first boarded the vessel had disappeared as soon as he saw the land speed by below him. It had been ten times faster than the vehicle he'd ridden in only hours before, and he'd thought that was fast! The technology that the Oflors had kept from the rest of Oryon was astounding, but he understood why they remained hidden. From his own standpoint, if his father were still alive and had known about it, he would not have hesitated to use whatever he could lay his hands on to destroy his rivals.

At that moment, seeing his world from way above it, he had a sudden epiphany. He had to do everything in his power to unite his world and to establish peace. He didn't know how he was going to go about it, but there was no question in his mind. Should the Zaruthrans or the Capricis win the war, Oryon would be laid to waste and in their kings' hands. The two clans might be presently united in their warmongering, but as soon as they decimated their enemies, they would turn on themselves. Should they lay claim to Oflor's technology, they would not only destroy each other but everything and everyone in their path.

Tarragon had closed his eyes and seen the future as clearly as if it were happening before him. He had no doubt that he would die for his people. He prayed to the Goddess and hoped she would listen to his plea. Although he had the talent as well as the mages of Oflor, somehow, he knew it wouldn't be enough. Now, as he stood by the Justice's ramps, urging his people aboard, he sent a prayer once more up to the Goddess.

Once they'd reached Dacron Palace, a message from Lucien came in, advising them to land just behind the temple. When they did, Brenn lowered the ramp, giving Tarragon and another soldier the order to guide the waiting men and women. Tarragon had never seen them before and concluded they must have been the ones Lucien's son had managed to get into the palace walls. There were no children as far as Tarragon could see, though there were several women who were obviously pregnant and frightened. Seeing them, Tarragon immediately embraced them in his mind, sending calming thoughts toward them, urging them to hurry. When at last there was no one left about, Tarragon signaled the soldier to close the ramp and hurried back to Brenn.

"Is everyone aboard?" Brenn asked over his shoulder as soon as the doors slid open.

"Yes, but I didn't see Lucien or Lawrence."

"I'm sure they're aboard one of the other ships. We need to hurry. The nearest Caprici forces are a day away, but we need to get out as soon as we can. We dare not delay."

Tarragon didn't argue. He strapped himself in the seat, feeling the Justice rise in a blast of air that sounded like thunder in his ears. Outside, through the glass opening in front of him, he saw the trees bend under the pressure of the vessel's engines. It was a marvelous sight to see, and Tarragon felt glad they hadn't met with any obstruction to save his people. Before him, the sunset washed the sky in brilliant golds and copper that deepened into a purple haze. He relaxed into his seat and sent up another prayer to the Goddess, this time in thanks. If he were to have a nightmare, it would be to awaken and find himself alive while the rest of his clan lay dead. As the king, he would most likely be killed, but the Capricis were malicious and cruel enough to keep him alive and use his people as slaves with no possibility of surviving. If he were to be given the chance to end this war, he knew he would have to be equally cruel, to eradicate the depravation of his enemies.

The Justice rose higher, and the sky deepened into a starlit night. Brenn sat quietly as he concentrated in his task of maneuvering his vessel. Everywhere else, it was quiet. Tarragon reached out with his mind and checked on the passengers, soothing those who were in pain or frightened. Not for the first time, he thanked the Goddess he had the talent to give his people reprieve. He closed his eyes and allowed his exhaustion to overcome him.

Then the Justice trembled and voices rose in cries of fear. Something exploded outside, and the Justice banked to its right. In a howl of engines, the vessel fought to stay up. The air snapped. Tarragon turned to see that Brenn had freed himself from his harness and had raised his hands.

Energy crackled and gathered around his forearms, momentarily poised over his palms, brightening the small space into a corona of bright light.

For a moment, Tarragon sat still, stunned at the display of power. And then he felt it. The Justice righted on itself, and the howling engines ceased. He could hear the wind howl around him.

"Tarragon!"

At Brenn's cry, Tarragon blinked himself out of his stupefaction and unstrapped himself. For a moment he stood, trying to think what it was he had to do, and then his mind opened, and he could hear the call of the engines. Without hesitation, he closed his eyes and willed the engines to life, feeling the energies rise in his body as he called forth the electricity that the machine could produce. From beside him, he heard Brenn's chuckle, and he smiled.

"Good. Good. Harness the energy, Tarr. Hold it in your mind like you would your people. Call to it . . . make it stronger."

Tarragon didn't question the instructions—he just did what he was told. As soon as he did so, he felt his body expand, as though he were bigger than the physical space that he stood in. He continued to call until he knew he had everything that he needed.

"What do you want me to do, Brenn?"

"Wrap the energies around the Justice, protect it from the attack outside. Hold it steady until I land us on safe ground."

Tarragon followed what he was asked to do, focusing on the electrical current until he could see it crawl from his arms onto the surfaces around him. Although it felt simple, Tarragon could feel the sweat form on his brow. He opened his eyes and met Brenn's gaze.

"I will let go now, Tarr. Hold it steady," Brenn said, violet lightning flashing in his eyes.

Tarragon gave a grim nod. "You can let go. I have everything under control."

Brenn threw him a grin before he took his seat once more and started punching on the controls in front of him. Tarragon heard the hiss of something fly at them. Acting on instinct, he gathered the forces for a moment before letting it go. On the surge of his magic, Tarragon focused his fury on the thing that was attacking them. He watched as his magic coalesced in his hands in a bright ball of purple electricity. He let it go in a flash of blue light that crawled its way out of the Justice and hit the object hurtling their way. When energy met mass, a flash of blue fire enveloped it until it melded and heated it to a searing red. Tarragon did not have time to rejoice, for behind the first object two others were flying

127

their way. In a scream of defiance, he hurled more of the electricity toward the first, then the second, watching as the searing light leaped out and hit them, making them expand. The explosions shook the Justice, and Tarragon was momentarily overtaken. But he soon righted himself and watched as the weapons fell back to the earth below them. Tarragon let out a puff of air, relieved he'd successfully deflected the weapons from the Justice. He paused to catch his breath. Exhausted, dizzy, and fighting against the vertigo that suddenly hit him, Tarragon widened his eyes and called forth the will of resolve. He had to continue fighting. He had to keep his people safe.

With a roar of defiance, he shrugged off the thick jacket he wore and took a deep breath. He called for the electricity once more, glad for its quick response. Holding the energies in place, he sent out his senses to check on his people and found them frightened but safe.

"Tarr, I hate to say this, but we need to land."

"Why? I can hold the energies . . . we can make it."

"No, I'm sorry, but we can't. We were hit, and we're losing fuel. I'll tell the other flyers to go ahead and send us help."

"What about the others with us?"

"They'll have to fight with us."

Tarragon met Brenn's gaze and saw that there was nothing he could do. He nodded grimly.

"All right, tell the others we're landing."

"Where?"

"Believe it or not, we're at Oflor's borders. They know we're here. We'll just have to wait for them to get to us."

CHAPTER NINETEEN

Tarragon cursed as another attacker beset him. He ducked when the man thrust a sword to his face, and he countered it with a single chop of his own sword into the throat of his enemy. The man fell, a death rattle escaping his lips as blood spilled from his wound. Precious seconds passed because Tarragon slipped in a pool of blood. Attempting to regain balance, he hissed out in pain when his ankle twisted. Finally freeing himself, he stepped over the body and limped forward, pain jabbing the length of his leg from ankle to thigh each time it bore his weight. The agony knotted in his belly and he swallowed to keep from vomiting. He mentally berated himself. After years of fighting the seemingly endless war, he should have learnt to watch where he stepped.

Hobbling headlong into another fight, he thrust out his hand and let go of the energies from his hand. Electricity met the metal shield on an enemy's arm in a resounding crackle and pop. The shield broke in half, allowing some of the energy to push itself through and strike home. The Zaruthran soldier went down, his dying eyes dimming in wide-eyed terror, the scent of burning flesh a mere side note on Tarragon's palate. He grimaced at the sight and smell of burning bodies.

"Brenn," Tarragon called out, his voice ringing clear. His gaze glossed over the blur of faces around him. He thought he spotted Brenn's tall frame and took a running step toward him when something hard hit him on his face.

129

"Tarragon!" Brenn's voice came across loudly, and Tarragon knew his loyal Guardian would come to his aid.

Attempting to rise to his feet, Tarragon panicked when he couldn't feel his legs. The clash of metal swelled all around and above him. He believed it was his soldiers defending him.

Love for his clan's people swelled in Tarragon's heart and mind. He held on to the emotion and willed it to bloom. If he could not fight physically, he would use his connection with his people to give them the boost they sorely needed. He knew morale had dropped the moment he had fallen. He had to let them know their leader was still with them. Such was the gift of the Dacron king.

On and on the shouting and the fighting went. Tarragon tried to open his eyes, and when his lids finally parted, his heart knew gladness. A figure in blue was shouting and pointing his sword above him. Brenn.

"The prince has fallen!" The voice of an attacking soldier shouted. Tarragon turned his head only to see Brenn beset with enemy soldiers. Through the haze of pain, he watched Brenn defend his fallen form. Above him, Brenn fought like a man gone amok, his face twisted in every shout of challenge and victory, his sword dripping with the blood of their enemies. He turned to the right and the left, turning on his feet like a dancer, his sword humming in a scream of speed and death by blade. Vaguely, Tarragon became aware of other soldiers coming to their aid, but try as he might, he couldn't do anything. He couldn't help his trusted Guardian. Crippled, he fought hard to remain conscious. In a moment of realization, he knew how he could help Brenn.

Forcing himself to take focus deep inside himself, he pulled on the last of his energies and pointed his hand toward Brenn. He watched as the energies crawled up his arm, slowly gathering on his hand until there was nothing left to give. With a word and a flick of the hand, whatever magic was left inside of him he gave freely to Brenn. Brenn didn't flinch when the energies entered his body. The only sign he gave was a renewed shout of challenge to the descending enemies. Brenn had honed his fighting skills before he'd been appointed Guardian by Tarragon. The years served him well in the minutes that passed as stroke after stroke, the sweat running in rivulets down his face, he defended Tarragon.

Blinking salty drops of blood and sweat from his eyes, Tarragon prayed to the Goddess. Everything around him blurred, the white haze of pain increased. Dimly, he heard the battle sounds around him fall to silence, and finally someone crouching over him, gentle hands pressing on him, a gentle voice calling his name.

Blinded by pain, Tarragon struggled to rise and failed. Someone told him to lie still even as another voice shouted for help. Tarragon reached out with numbed fingers toward Brenn, conscious that with even that slightest of movements, he was losing sight. He gasped, but no air entered his lungs. His fingers dug in the dirt around him and he struggled to rise.

"Do not move, sire." Brenn's voice sounded gritty and desperate.

Not wanting to distress his Guardian, Tarragon did as he was told and relaxed in the arms that held him.

"Hang on, sire. Aid is coming," Brenn whispered in his ear.

Tarragon wanted to say something, to assure his man that he was going to be all right, but he couldn't. He knew life was draining from him. He offered up a smile to Brenn, but in his mind, he invoked another prayer to the Goddess, this time, willing for his own death. His only remorse was that he had no one to give up his memories to. Just like he'd not received them from his father. How could he have? War had left him no chance to find someone who would bear him his children.

Blurred shapes swam in and out of his focus and time slowed down. Through the fog of death, he felt Brenn's hand grasp his and hold it tight. Tarragon frowned and wondered what was to happen to his people. He had done his best to defeat their enemies and had used his magic, risked being found out a mage. But there had been too many, and without his father's memories to aid him in tactical warfare, he was simply too inexperienced against them. Oh, how he wished he had more time left, if only to see them kneel to the Dacron.

Such was not to be.

"Brenn," he muttered softly.

"Yes, sire," Brenn said, holding him tighter against his chest.

"Guard my clan well, my loyal Guardian," Tarragon breathed out, just before the earth beneath him overturned. Vertigo hit him, and he slipped into the abyss.

Sounds intruded.

Through the thick darkness, Tarragon heard voices. They echoed through his dreams, swimming against the unforgiving pain. He didn't know how it was that he could hear these voices, for he was sure he had died in Brenn's arms.

" . . . I don't care what you say. I want you to save him."

Even from the depths of the abyss, Tarragon recognized the voice. It was Brenn.

"I will not allow you not to do anything . . ."

"It is too late. He is at the shadow's door . . . serious his wounds are . . . infected . . . his energy depleted . . . his life force almost non-existent . . ."

"There is another way." Tarragon did not recognize the

third voice.

"How? Tell me how and I will do it." Brenn sounded desperate.

Tarragon wanted to reassure his loyal Guardian that everything was going to be all right, but when he tried to open his mouth, it was as though his tongue was tied. "Brenn," Tarragon murmured. "No."

A bustle in the darkness, and then he felt Brenn's hand in his. There was a curious sound, and Tarragon fought hard to try to analyze it.

"Tarragon! My king!"

He heard the same sound once again and immediately knew that it was coming from Brenn. It sounded like his Guardian was crying.

"He has enough life force left in him. Maybe it will work," that third voice said.

"Tarragon?" Brenn's voice said again. This time Tarragon knew Brenn was close, for the words had been spoken by his ear. Cool hands brushed his brow. The fingers were rough, but they were trembling.

And then a light shone. It was blinding in its brightness, and Tarragon flinched back and closed his eyes. Consciousness flooded back, along with the full awareness of pain throughout his body. He couldn't contain the moan escaping his lips.

"Tarragon," Brenn said once again. His hands settled on either side of Tarragon's temples. Gently, insistently, they framed his face. Tarragon slowly opened his eyes and met the violet gaze of his Guardian.

"You may punish me once you are well enough, but you need to know that we were able to defeat our ambushers. However, you've been wounded, and I had no other choice. I broke all protocol and brought you to the mages. I'll apologize for keeping my knowledge of their whereabouts from you later, once you're better. Right now, you must focus on staying awake. You've lost a lot of blood, and you've exhausted your magic. You don't have long to live, but we think we have found a way for you to survive. All I need from you is your permission. Will you allow me to save your people? Save us all?"

CHAPTER TWENTY

Through the haze of pain, Tarragon managed to focus his eyes. Brenn bent over him, his dark hair loosely hanging on either side of his face. But it was his eyes that Tarragon focused on. Those beautiful and unique violet eyes that had never failed to fascinate him. It was a truly wondrous color. He was near the shadows, but the Goddess was not welcoming him as yet. Tarragon drew in a difficult breath, one that burned through his nostrils and down his throat. His lungs thirsted for the air they desperately needed, and he hissed in agony when only a tiny amount entered them.

"Brenn. I am dying."

Brenn stroked down his cheek. "Yes. You are. But, if you would allow me, you may just yet live. There is no guarantee what we are about to do will work."

Tarragon thought back to the sounds of fighting before he had collapsed. He remembered his promise to his people — that he would do everything in his power to end the war and unite Oryon.

"What chance?"

Brenn shook his head. "I cannot say. Every time we've tried, it never worked."

"How many?"

"How many times have we tried?"

Tarragon nodded.

Brenn's lips tightened into a thin line. "Too many."

Tarragon swallowed hard and gave a brief, grim nod.

"Thank you," Brenn breathed out.

The others around them breathed audible sighs of relief. Tarragon didn't understand why they would. He knew he was dying, but he had to give them a last bit of hope. Even for just a little while. And then he would sleep in the shadows. The last thought made him regret his failure. If only he had been stronger. If only he'd had the knowledge. If only.

Brenn's hands fumbled as he let go of Tarragon, but then he moved his arms beneath Tarragon's body and lifted him in his arms. Tarragon lost consciousness.

When he woke up again, he was once more on his back, but this time, the stars above were moving. He realized he was on a litter.

"My prince? How are you feeling?" Brenn was walking beside him, his left hand on the hilt of his sword and his right holding on to Tarragon's hands.

"More dead than alive," Tarragon managed to say.

"More alive than dead, I would say, if you can answer so flippantly."

"How?"

Brenn gave a brief smile. "I lent you some of my energies."

"How?"

Brenn met his gaze. "You may be young and not know how to use your talent, but believe it or not, you've got quite the talent. I am not as powerful as you, my king, but I have enough knowledge and use of my talent to be able to share my energies with you. You're far from healed, your body is just too injured, but it was enough."

"Enough for what?"

"Enough for you to get to where we need to take you."

Tarragon let out a breath of impatience. Surprisingly, his lungs didn't burn, and he actually felt a little stronger.

"Will you stop with the cryptic replies and just answer me

straight, soldier?"

"Oh, I think I've been demoted," Brenn said, his shoulders shaking lightly.

"Answer me!"

Brenn fussed over him when Tarragon started to cough. "You shouldn't get over emotional, sire. Save your strength."

"Where are we going? What are we going to?"

Brenn fixed Tarragon's blanket over his chest before straightening. His hand never left Tarragon's. "There is a prophecy that in a time of great war, when all hope is lost, a mage would be born of a royal line. He alone will have the strength and will to survive all his foes. That he alone will hear the roar of life and wield the energies with a strength never seen before. That on the brink of hopelessness, he will rise and secure a legacy that will never die. He would be immortal." Brenn stopped speaking and looked down once more at Tarragon. "We believe you are that princely mage."

"All right, let's say this prophecy of yours is true. How is it going to happen?"

Brenn smiled. The expression on his face was one of tenderness and a whole lot of hope.

"I have no idea. But I know how to get there. I know what to do. The outcome, whatever it may be, is all up to the Goddess."

Tarragon could only stare. He dared not say what he thought. Brenn was a great warrior of a soldier, but right that minute, Tarragon thought he was either insane or had a whole lot of faith on the Goddess. He hoped it was the latter. He let out a sigh and closed his eyes.

"Wake me up when we get there," he whispered.

Brenn didn't speak, but his hold on Tarragon's hand tightened.

Later Tarragon became aware of a stillness that enveloped him. He felt at peace, and other than the pain returning, everything was quiet. Forcing himself to open his eyes, he saw that he was no longer on the litter. He now lay on a mat, and above him was a stone ceiling. Looking about, he saw that he had been set in the middle of what appeared to be a chamber of stone. He wasn't entirely sure if he was in a cave or a manmade room. The walls were bare, and except for a faint, greenish light that cast shadows everywhere he looked, he was alone.

Tarragon closed his eyes once more, exhaustion screaming from every muscle and joint, overriding the waves of pain that seemed to be staging a comeback. Despite the knowledge that he was going to die, he felt content. At least he had given Brenn the last bit of hope he seemed to need desperately.

But then, something ... called, and consciousness wavered. He heard no sound, but he could hear the something as clearly as a bell ringing in between his ears. It continued to call to him, its tone getting excited.

"Who's there?"

Whatever or whoever it was out there, Tarragon couldn't tell, for darkness claimed him.

He didn't know how long he had lost consciousness, but when he next opened his eyes, he was aware of the lack of pain. He'd gotten used to feeling his body scream, and its absence confused him.

Tarragon opened his eyes and became even more confused by how easily he'd done so. Of late, it had become an effort to lift his eyelids. He also realized he heard no buzzing between his ears, nor was there blurriness to his vision. In fact, he felt better than he had in ages.

He rolled his head and felt his spine pop, spreading welcome relief through his muscles. He wondered if Brenn had thought to lend him his energies again and thought to reprimand the man. He didn't know how that would affect Brenn's body and had never read any reports or research results of a study. His muscles felt tight, so Tarragon stretched out his arms, relishing the pull. When he finally set down his arms, he felt refreshed . . . and curiously stronger.

"Damn it. This endless waiting is killing me. Why won't you allow me to go inside and find out how he is doing? What if he's dead, or in pain?"

Tarragon looked up at the sound of Brenn's voice. Before he could call out a reply, another voice interjected. The voice sounded distressed.

"We have to let him be! That is what the prophecy instructs us. We don't know if it will work or not, but we can't do anything to interrupt the process. The prophecy says to leave the contender in the room at least three days."

"But what if it doesn't work? How do we know if it works or not? I need to get in there. I need to know if Tarragon's still alive."

"Did you feel the separation?" the other voice snapped. There was a sound of a hand striking flesh. "Get a hold of yourself. You are a soldier and a mage. You should know that we cannot interfere with something which we know nothing about. You need to trust in the prophecy."

"Shut up! Both of you shut up!" a third voice broke in. And then the three voices merged together in a sound of angry discourse. Their tones rose and fell like waves that echoed in the room.

Tarragon lay still, listening to Brenn's upset voice argue with the two others. Despite the loud angry tones, Tarragon recognized that the two other voices were just as distressed as Brenn. He didn't know why he couldn't just stand up and appease their pain. Long minutes passed until finally the voices were silent.

And then the second voice spoke up. "Brenn, it will do none of us good if we continue to fight one another. I know it pains you not knowing how the king is, but we don't have any choice. The records are quite clear. Those who entered the cave and sought to interrupt the process not only died, but they suffered for it. In any case, there are only a few hours left before the doors open."

Tarragon swallowed hard. Although the agony from his wounds was gone, he was aware that something else was wrong with him.

Well, not wrong. There was the absence of pain, and he could wiggle his toes and fingers. Also, he felt really, really good. Only he felt different. Stronger, but not quite. And curiously refreshed. It was as though he had taken a long, hot bath and had slept on a comfortable bed. He couldn't remember the last time he'd had a proper bath or slept on a proper bed.

So why was he feeling as though he had?

CHAPTER TWENTY-ONE

"His people need to know! Don't you understand that? He has been gone far longer than we expected. We thought he would only be gone for three or four days. Lorta, it's gone two weeks. The Zaruthra troops have declared him dead. The Capricis have celebrated their victory! Tarragon's value lies in his presence. If they don't see him soon, standing there for all to see, the clan will assume the worst."

Silence followed Brenn's speech.

As Tarragon waited, lying under the cave ceiling, he examined his surroundings. Other than the ceiling, he could see nothing resembling a cave at all. In fact, if he hadn't known he'd entered one, he would have thought that he was inside some sort of laboratory — though there seemed to be a lack of equipment.

Back home, his father had never encouraged their scientists to work on their theories and invent machines that would benefit their clan. Tarragon knew that even if he had, they would never have reached the heights which the Kayels had achieved. His father even had to purchase the generators, outdated ones, but they hadn't known that then.

As a young boy, Tarragon had felt drawn to the rooms, but those who worked there had always shooed him away, saying he was too young to be in there. Of course, when his father found out, he'd been reprimanded severely. Tarragon had learned to sneak around the backs of his guards so he could observe the wonders of the laboratories hidden in the shadows.

Time moved slowly, and Tarragon observed it from a distance. He looked down and saw his body lying prone on a stone slab. Objectively, he looked at the design. It was obviously fabricated—the lines were too straight and the angles too sharp to have been hewn by sand and wind. Also, there was no wind going through the cave, although the temperature was comfortable. He frowned and peered into the far end of the cavern. The same sort of technology that had made the stone table had cut out this room into a perfectly rectangular shape, at least by his analysis. And what about that curious green light? Tarragon couldn't figure out its source, and yet it managed to illuminate the room, making it easy to see around.

Tarragon cocked his head to the side. He couldn't quite figure out why he was looking down at his body. He knew he wasn't dead, and yet here he was, floating about, as though he were . . . dead. No, not dead. More like . . . observing from another set of eyes?

That last realization surprised him, and when next he blinked, he found himself staring up at the ceiling. He tried to move his arm and found that he could. He frowned at the ease with which he flexed his arm. Last he remembered, he had been hacked there by one of his attackers.

A weary sort of fog descended over him, and he relaxed in its embrace.

When Tarragon next opened his eyes, it was in reaction to a disturbance coming from his left. He opened one eye and looked in the direction.

Entering the room were three men who looked vaguely familiar. Leading them was Brenn. His violet eyes blazed brightly in the dim green illumination, and his form threw dark shadows on the walls. He strode determinedly straight to where Tarragon lay. He shot a glance toward the men who followed him.

"Get out," he said. "I want to talk to the king alone, see what he thinks about you keeping him from his clan."

Tarragon looked up into Brenn's face and immediately saw the anxiety behind the fury. He forced himself not to reveal his amusement and keep his voice as firm as he could without laughing.

"You're a bit impertinent, aren't you, my loyal Guardian. Were I not still lying on this table, I would discipline you."

Brenn shrugged and leaned over him, a tender smile hovering over his lips. He raised a hand and raked it through Tarragon's hair.

"If you had the strength to stand up and discipline me, sire, I would gladly kneel and let you." He caught Tarragon's gaze and held it before straightening and crossing his arms over his chest. "I see that you are looking much better, not pale and wan-looking like a walking cadaver."

Tarragon huffed. "I am not a walking dead, Brenn, nor do I plan to be. But you're correct—I am feeling a lot better. Stronger, too, if you really want to know."

"Then why are you still lying there as though you are getting ready to cross over to the shadows? One might think you were languishing, for all the risks we took to get you back on your feet."

"I was thinking of staying here for a little longer," Tarragon said, consciously masking his amusement.

"Your people need to see you. They need to know that their king is still alive."

"They know I'm alive, Brenn. I haven't relinquished my hold over their psyches."

"Well, I know that, but the Zaruthrans and the Capricis don't know it and are spreading word that you are dead or dying."

"I'm sure they can do without me, Brenn, at least, just for

a little while longer. I have served my people more than my family ever has."

"I'm sorry, my king, but I cannot agree to that. You have to stand up and show them you are alive. Knowing you are alive is far different from seeing for themselves that you are in fact alive and breathing." Brenn closed his eyes, as though struggling to get the words out. "Your people are left with no king to guide them. You have neither generals nor master tacticians, not the way your father or your brothers had."

"No, I only have you and Lucien for now."

"Yes, you only have us." Brenn frowned, then with obvious discomfort, rushed on. "Your father may have been king, but he was vain and idiotic. He refused to recognize those who were better than he or more talented than he was. He did not approve for those beneath his station to sound or look more intelligent than he was, either. Those generals of his were for dress only." Brenn flushed and looked deep into Tarragon's eyes. "It was why he kept your training from you and always belittled you. Your eldest brother, Magnus, saw your talent and made sure that you were trained. Unfortunately, he acted too late and died before he could guarantee your real training."

Tarragon frowned. He didn't know why he said the next thing he said, but he did. "Who do you think you are to judge my father?"

Brenn flushed, a dark red rising to his cheeks. He clenched his fists before turning to Tarragon once more. His jaw worked as though he were gritting his teeth.

"You know I'm right," Brenn said in an accusing voice. "To continue losing more of your people through the stupidity of incompetent generals deprived our people our victory and our lives. If you want things to remain as they have, I am not staying around to see you destroy our clan. Go ahead, seek the easy way out, but heed my warning. Now that you know I am a mage, I need you to know the facts of it. Yes, I am what I am, but you also seem to forget that I am a Master Mage. I am the only one who is. My father and I, we risked our people for you. I made sure you were kept safe from the Zaruthrans and the Capricis, whose only wish is for your line to die out. Your father's enemies are simply waiting for the right moment to swoop over Oryon and take over everything and every person who relies on your strength to keep their wills up. I made sure you survived your father. Cut me down now and kill me if you think I will allow you to give up what we have both been fighting for.

"I love you, Tarragon. Not just because you are my lover or you are my king, but because I know what you are capable of. I also know you are the fulfillment of the prophecy that I and my family have been waiting for, for generations. Do not disappoint me. Do not fail your people."

Before Tarragon could think of a comeback, Brenn was gone.

Something inside him groaned and moaned its disappointment. Around him, the green light dimmed, and for a brief moment, it was as though time had stood still. A sigh of disappointment from the doorway drew Tarragon's attention, and belatedly he realized that the three men who had followed Brenn inside earlier had not left despite his orders.

When Tarragon saw their expressions, a feeling of guilt swept through him.

"I was only teasing him, you know?"

One of the men stepped closer. "No, Your Highness, I did not know. Neither did Lorta and Jordan. And, if I am not mistaken, neither did Master Brenn."

Tarragon frowned. "Do you have to call him Master? He's my Guardian."

The man gave a brief smile. "Because he is the Master Mage, sire. Didn't you listen to what he said to you?"

"How can he be a Master? Isn't he too young to have accomplished that status? I mean, he's told me, but I still can't believe it."

"A master is someone who is born with the talent, young king. Just as you were born with your talent. You have the potential to be a master, but Brenn was born with his mastery and skill. Once in every generation, a master is born among us, and we make sure to protect him until he becomes of age. When he reached his majority, Brenn looked to the Dacron and predicted your birth. When he was proven right, he left us and sought employment as a soldier so he could watch over you."

"He told me that. He also told me that he was eighty years old. That's hard to believe. He looks my age, and I'm only eighteen."

"He's telling you the truth, sire."

"I'd heard that mages lived longer lives than us ordinary people," Tarragon said, looking toward where Brenn had disappeared. "I guess I have to apologize to him."

"That can wait," the man said. "We need to examine you, find out if the merge was completed."

Tarragon frowned. "What merge? What are you talking about?"

"They're talking about your symbiont, Tarragon."

Tarragon looked around and saw that Brenn had reentered the room. His face was devoid of expression, his tone even, but Tarragon knew him well enough to read the anger in his stance. His hands, hidden in his back, were most likely gripped so tightly the knuckles would whiten under the pressure.

"Allow Lorta to examine you. We don't have much time before you are presented before your people." Brenn motioned sharply with his head, signaling Lorta to approach.

Tarragon let out a sigh. "Why must you continually interfere? I don't need anyone to tell me how I'm feeling. I feel perfectly well. I don't know what happened or what you did to me, but it helped. I'm happy to tell you that I'm not dying, Brenn."

If it was at all possible, Brenn's features darkened even more. "If I have any quarrel with you, sire, is that you don't take your health seriously. Lorta *will* examine you, and *you* will *not* object to whatever tests he runs on you."

Tarragon rolled his eyes and in one breath, sat up.

Brenn didn't even bat an eye, but the tic on the corner of his mouth betrayed his surprise. Or was it frustration?

Tarragon didn't care. He swung his legs over the side of the stone platform and jumped to his feet. "Look, I'm fine, see?" He swung his arms out and turned around slowly.

"What I see is a spoiled young king who thinks he's invincible. You're not. No matter what you think or feel, you can still get hurt. You may be up and about, but we still need to know how your body is healing. The wound in your leg may seem fine, but as it was nearly cut in two just two days ago, I doubt if you can honestly suggest that it is a hundred percent healed." Brenn narrowed his eyes, his gaze locked with Tarragon's.

Tarragon's shoulders sagged. He recognized that look.

"Sire, perhaps if you could take a seat? I can examine you quicker, and then you can go on with whatever it is you have in mind you want to do." Lorta bowed diffidently. His tone was respectful enough, but Tarragon also didn't miss the slight curl on the corner of his lips.

Tarragon let out a resigned sigh, cast a smile toward Brenn and walked the three steps toward the chair beside the platform. Lorta walked over to him.

"Sire, if you please? Can you extend your arm?"

"So, how long have I been asleep?" Tarragon watched as Lorta palpated his left arm. He was sure it had been hacked in three places, but, other than the torn sleeve, there was no sign of the injury. There was not even a scratch on his skin.

"We entered these caves eighteen days ago," Brenn said.

Tarragon looked up sharply. "I heard you arguing earlier. I don't know with whom. I thought I heard you say that you hadn't been able to see me since I got in here. Did I hear right?"

"That argument happened a week ago. Lorta and Jordan stopped me from entering."

"Ah," was all Tarragon said.

Lorta signaled to his other arm and Tarragon did as requested. "I thought it would have been them. Why couldn't you come see me?"

"The last time someone interrupted the joining ceremony, all were found dead at the entrance of the cave. Including one prince."

"Did you thank them for saving your life?"

"No," Brenn said shortly.

"Why not?"

"Because I don't want to. Any other questions?"

Tarragon didn't rise to the challenge in Brenn's voice. He recognized belligerence when he heard it.

"When was the last time this particular ceremony was attempted?" he asked after a minute.

"Too long," Lorta said as he straightened. "Sire, I will examine your back now."

"How long?" Save for a nod of assent, Tarragon ignored Lorta, his gaze set on Brenn's.

Brenn met Tarragon's gaze, his jaw working on his cheek. "Two hundred years ago."

"I see," Tarragon said. He leaned forward when Lorta asked him to and lifted his shirt to expose his back.

"Do you even know what's going on? What Lorta is looking for?"

"Hmm," Lorta said.

Tarragon looked over his shoulder as he tried to see what Lorta had found. "What is it?"

"Master Brenn, could you come over here, please. I need to show you something," Lorta said instead.

Quickly, Brenn walked up to stand behind Tarragon. Tarragon continued to look over his shoulder, and when both men didn't say anything, he huffed in annoyance.

"Will one of you please tell me what's going on?"

CHAPTER TWENTY-TWO

Tarragon walked slowly among the cluster of flowers. They were everywhere, and their scent filled the night air. The sight of the rich and fertile gardens had surprised him at first, but after walking through their maze and feeling his anger ebb away, he understood why the mages had placed it there. After learning what had happened to him, what Brenn had done to him, rage at Brenn's duplicity had made him act out in anger. He'd always been told, from the first moments of his memory, that he was never to bare his emotions to anyone other than his mirror in the privacy of his bedroom. As a child, seeing the stoic expressions of his older brothers and father, he only now appreciated the wisdom of keeping emotions at bay.

For men in his position, there were times when decisions had to be made that were neither popular nor considered gentle, decisions that would mean the life or death of one man, or one thousand soldiers. Lately, there were times that he'd wished for the luxurious openness of the common person. He wondered how it would have felt to simply let go and cry, allow the tears to fall unchecked, without fear of being judged a weakling. A coward.

I'm sorry you found out that way.

Tarragon stumbled in his steps at the sound of the voice. It came from inside his head. The first time he'd heard it speak, he'd thought that one of the mages had come into the cave. Seeing no one had got him thinking that he and Brenn were in danger. But when it had spoken again, and he'd seen that neither Brenn nor Lorta had heard the speech, he'd thought he'd gone insane. And then the voice had crooned to him, immediately gentling his anxiety. When it showed him images of their joining, he'd lost control and would forever deny it from having happened.

He had fainted.

It was a good thing Brenn was there to catch you. I would have had to fix you again.

"Can you please just . . . stop!" Tarragon raised his palms before him.

Stop what? Speaking to you?

"Yes! Stop talking to me!"

And when do you want me to speak to you again? A huff similar to that of a snort of derision echoed in his mind. *Do you know how long I've had to wait for the right candidate?*

Tarragon blinked, for the thought had never occurred to him. "Uhm . . . I don't know?"

Another scoff and a huff. *Eight hundred years, Tarragon. Eight hundred of your years.*

"That's not my fault!"

I am not saying that it's your fault, you silly child.

"Gah! I am not a child!" Tarragon gripped his hair in his hands and gave it a pull. He welcomed the pain. It made him think he was still sane.

Will you please stop overreacting? You sound like a spoiled little boy who's angry because he can't get what he wanted. And for your information, I may have waited forever for you to come to me, but I can sincerely tell you that you are a great disappointment.

Tarragon gasped out, his mouth falling open. He glared at the gardens and the stars above him.

"How dare you!"

Ahh, there he goes again. Now you're making me regret thinking you were the right partner for me. A regretful sigh followed by a grumble filled Tarragon's mind. *I was so looking forward to finally joining with a worthy partner, and I get . . . a toddler.*

"You take that back!" Tarragon punched the air, turning on an ankle as he did so. He felt foolish.

You can stop shouting for a start, and then I'll think of taking back . . . wait. What did you want me to take back? I don't under-stand. Did I give you something other than — oh! Now I remember. I just saved your life, didn't I? Hmm, do you want me to leave you so you can die? Again?

Tarragon stilled, his frustration fading. "What do you mean again?"

A sigh echoed in his mind. *You died, Tarragon. You needed to die before I could join with you. It's how things are with my kind.*

Tarragon's mouth dropped open. He was at a loss for words. He tried to process what whoever it was inside his mind had just told him. He came up empty. Blinking rapid-ly, he looked around him until he spotted a bench, his knees feeling weak. He needed to sit down. His palms felt sweaty, so he wiped them over his thighs. Then his palms began to feel itchy, and he scratched at them. He was nervous, and he didn't know why. When he reached the stone bench, he sat and leaned his elbows over his knees. The breeze rose around him, bringing with it a myriad of fragrances from the flowers all around him. He looked up to the sky, reveling in the millions of stars twinkling in the night sky. If he didn't feel so anxious and nervous, he would have lain on the ground so he could enjoy the quiet and maybe have a good cry. But his situation was different.

How different can it be? You can still enjoy the stars just like any other day, or night. Take a deep breath and relax. You'll find that it will be all for the best. Myself, I really like your night skies. This world is so different from mine, and yet it is alike.

Tarragon closed his eyes and shook his head. He was so confused. So. He wasn't insane, but he had to find out what had happened. First things first.

"Who are you really?"

I am Onik.

"What are you?"

I am Hobik.

Tarragon had never heard of a Hobik before. To him, it sounded like a small and cute looking animal, but somehow, that didn't feel right. Not with the deep and powerful sound of the creature's voice inside his head.

"What is a Hobik exactly and where do you come from?"

The creature grumbled. It sounded hesitant, as if it didn't know how to proceed in answering his question.

How tired are you?

Tarragon blinked back his surprise. "I'm all right. Not too tired. Though, I could use some food."

All right, why don't we go back to your fellow. I felt his curiosity earlier. He may be a master in his craft, but he does not have the answers. Truthfully, no one has the answers.

"Who has them? You?"

Yes. Only I can provide you the answers. But the process is long, and it can be painful. I need you to be strong. With your fellow, you will have the emotional support to withstand the information.

"You make it sound like I'm in danger."

You are. In a way. I need you strong, and I haven't yet had the time to completely heal you.

"Heal me? What are you talking about? I thought the mages were the ones who took care of me."

Please, have patience. Come. Let us join your fellow and get you something to eat. I haven't tasted any food since I ended up on this planet of yours and I am feeling . . . needy.

Tarragon's stomach grumbled loudly, and he had a sudden urge to run back into the caves and seek meat. The image of biting into hot, fresh flesh overwhelmed his senses. All of a sudden, he knew what was happening to him was not normal.

"Are you responsible for making me suddenly feeling so

hungry I want to run inside and eat anything?"

Yes. Now come. I am in need of food. It's been ages for me.

CHAPTER TWENTY-THREE

Tarragon found himself standing in front of a wide window. Outside, he could see an immense city of towers. Everywhere he looked, he saw structures and open sky, a sky so deeply red, he found himself squinting to see through the dim light. He stepped closer to the window until he saw his breath cloud the glass. He looked down and saw that he was standing in a tall building, and below it, there was the haze. He didn't know what caused it or where it came from. It looked to be coming from everywhere. He looked up and saw dense clouds.

Something flashed outside, and he turned to look at it. He didn't see anything, but the haze could have caused that. From his side, something shimmered, and he squinted in that direction, only to decide that it was lights blinking faintly in the distance. Between each of the buildings were connecting bridges. Tiny figures walked the lengths, to and fro, going he didn't know where. Everything looked so alien and forbidding.

Where am I? What is this place?

My home planet, or at least, it was. What you are seeing is a memory. Shimra is no more. Onik's voice sounded full of longing.

What happened? How did it get destroyed?

Expecting a snarky reply, Tarragon flinched when the images rolled back and rushed into his mind. He gasped and took several steps back when the explosion of images crowded his mind. And just as he regained his balance, the sensory attack stopped. There was a stillness about him, an absence of any sort of sound or feeling, and yet it was as though he were caught in the middle of a storm. Once more, he opened his eyes, and just like before, the panorama before him extended beyond what his eyes should see, and yet, he could.

He turned and saw that no longer was he standing in a room. Instead, the wind began to howl around him. It carried with it suggestions of the unknown. From the left, he felt the gust of heated air, reminding him of forests and rich, lush earth. It also carried with it the smell of rushing water, of animals that swam in the deep, and of fertile lands that grew bountiful harvests. From his right, the gust of cold air made the hair on his arms stand on their ends. It brought with it the smell of ice and storms, and of the impossible crackle of energy. Behind him, he heard laughter of unbridled joy. The voices were not what he was used to, their deep, booming, thunderous sound too alien for him to comprehend, and yet it gave him the image of a young mother singing a lullaby to a child. It was all so confusing, and yet familiar.

Tarragon shivered, partly frightened, partly excited, partly anxious. To his front, he smelled the unique scents of spices — sweet, nutty, warm, and salty. He licked his lips and swore he could taste it all. He breathed in deeply and savored the different textures of the world he was being shown.

He turned, and Tarragon found himself atop a mountain. Gone were the cities that had been shown to him. Now he found himself shivering under the heat of a dying sun. Squinting, he looked up and saw the once red sun had faded to a pale pink. He frowned.

I don't understand.

You are seeing the death of my world.

But the cities.

Those are long gone now.

When?

Millions of years.

But you said you've been waiting for me for eight hundred years.

Yes.

I don't understand.

Onik grumbled, and Tarragon felt him settle in his mind. He was silent for a long time, and Tarragon thought he was not going to answer when he felt Onik shake himself back to the present. *It took me a millennia to find this planet. As I neared it, I felt its pull, and I sensed that this was where I would find my kind's future.*

I don't understand.

I am the last of my kind, Tarragon. When I set out on my journey, my partner sacrificed himself so I would last the time apart from him.

But you're still alive.

Yes. Thanks to Katalan, I made it through time and space.

Katalan?

My partner. What you are to me, he once was.

How?

He and the others made sure that in my body, I would carry all of the Hobik's seed.

Tarragon frowned. *You mean without you, your kind would become extinct?*

Yes. However, only a warrior class like myself could have made the journey. As I was the strongest of my kind, I was chosen to carry the future of my people.

What about Katalan? Was he a Hobik too?

No. He was Qratan. He was his people's greatest general. We had been together most of our lives, but he chose to give me his life energy so as to give me more chances of making it.

He sacrificed himself so you might live.

Yes. As well as the other Qratani and their Hobiks. We all knew it was the end for our world. By binding their energies to me, they ensured I and our kind would have a better chance.

What happened to your planet?

Once more, Tarragon flinched from the onslaught of images. He screamed from the sheer pressure of it, then opened his eyes to see the terror. Once more he found himself on an alien landscape, standing in the middle of what looked like a majestic cavern. Above him, he could hear the deep tones of a language he could not quite comprehend, and yet somehow, he did. People were hurriedly moving about, but there was no sense of panic. He took a step forward and looked down the edge of the platform he was standing on. Flame red and glowing, liquid rock seeped from the stones on the lower edges. Although Tarragon could sense their terror, the people were focused on the tasks they had been assigned to do. They ignored the lines of energy that pulsed their way from beneath the earth's crust. He didn't understand how these people could still go about their tasks, knowing their world was about to be destroyed at any moment. A grumbling roar tearing across the cavern made Tarragon look up. Terror rose at the sight before him. Gigantic in form, an animal the likes of which he'd never seen before barked out instructions to those around him.

It was gargantuan, with a head much like that of a *septurecce.* He couldn't see if there were teeth hidden within its pointed snout, but the jaw looked strong beneath its scales. It was golden in color, but when it moved, the scales rippled to a different color, and then another and another. Red, silver, green, black, and yellow, the different colors rippled across the creature's back. It moved and its tail curled around its bulk, a groan of despair echoed as it did so. It was a dragon, or at least, that was what Tarragon thought a dragon would look like.

No one paused, but as one, everyone tilted their heads in agreement. The animal roared once more, but this time, there was an anguish, a terror in its tone. A man, or what Tarragon could only assume was a man, stepped up and lay a caressing hand down the dragon's jaw. The dragon grumbled and whined, and Tarragon felt the fear coursing through it. It was saying goodbye. It knew this would be the end for it, and yet, it had hope. It looked down at Tarragon, and its eyes blinked.

Tarragon blinked as well, but then hot, harsh winds slammed into his chest, and the world began to crumble around him. His knees buckled, and he found himself kneeling on the edge of a platform. His heart fell at the sight of the endless pit before him. The vision wavered and pulled, compelling Tarragon to give everything up and jump. Carefully, he backed up, using his hands and knees to recover his balance. A surge of vertigo hit him, and he fell once more. Inside him, a familiar voice cried out. Somehow, he recognized it. Katalan.

—*Now. The time has come. Go, Onik! Do not falter. Live!*

Tarragon paused, momentarily confused. He was Onik. *I can't leave you!*

You must, my symbiont. You must. Only with you can our kind flourish.

But why can't you come with me? I cannot lose you.

I will always be with you, my symbiont. Now go! It is time. Stay strong, my brave Onik. Cross the universe, find the prophesied one. Find him. Teach him what he must know. Pass on the knowledge to the one who will bring us back.

Tarragon bowed his head as tears fell down his cheeks. With a roar of surrender, Onik sped through the conduit one of the mages had opened.

Blackness enveloped him, but he persevered. For Katalan, he would do anything. He flew through the vastness of space leaving behind him all that he knew, all that he loved. Within him, something called, and he sang to it. Soon. Soon, he would find the one whom he was sent out for. Soon, he would lay the eggs his kind had created and placed inside him so the Hobiks would live on. Soon, he would rest and find peace. Soon, he would find the undying one. The Immortal.

Chapter Twenty-four

He floated. He was Onik. He was Tarragon. He didn't know what, who, or where he was. All he knew was that he should save himself, prevent himself from drowning in the vacuum of space. He was afloat in a bubble of magic that only the most powerful of the mages of his kind could create. A magic that would have most probably been their last hurrah.

Why? Why didn't they just all leave? Why did they have to act the fools and think they would survive an exploding planet? Then again, he knew why. It was because their kind had been locked in that planet with their partners, the ones they had been dependent on to survive for much longer than any of their history could imagine. They had known no other world except Idrisi. What made him so different?

A voice from memory replied.

You are the first and the last of our kind. Our beginning from our end.

Onik huffed. *You made me what I am.*

The voice laughed. There was no joy to the sound. *It is good that you realize this.*

But why did I have to leave without Katalan? He was my everything, and now I am lost.

You will never be lost. You are made of much sterner stuff, Onik. You have been designed to withstand the absence of a symbiont for as long as your body remains in stasis. Our kind have never been able to survive without our partners.

But I love . . . loved him. He was my life.

You're wrong. He was but a temporary vessel so we may live on. Within you are the seed of our kind. Where we never had a choice on who our partners would be, you and the rest will have that choice.

Onik wondered how it could be so. *How are they to know? How will I know who will be the right partners?*

A mental caress soothed Onik's anxiety. *Only you will know. Only you and your kind will make the choice.*

Will they be good enough? Onik crooned. He would miss the Qratani, the only family he'd known and loved.

You will be the only one who could answer that question. Be well, Onik. A final mental caress, and then the memory faded.

A note echoed in the vastness of space. Tarragon turned and found himself moving faster than his mind could comprehend. Galaxies passed by, ignored. *What is that? Why is it pulling me to it?*

That is the sound of your destiny, the voice replied.

Will it love me? Such a youngling he was. But he needed to know.

He will.

Tarragon blinked back to reality, both sad and relieved he was back on the ground. What he had just witnessed was both terrifying and exhilarating. Was that going to be Oryon's future? To spread its wings beyond their planet? Oh, the wonder of it all made Tarragon's heart thunder in his chest. That, out there, the vastness of space — that was going to be his children's future. He would make sure of it.

"Brenn! I should go tell Brenn," Tarragon said, turning around to sprint across the uneven ground. He slowed down, his excitement fading, when Onik sighed inside his mind. It was a melancholy sound. "What is it?"

Brenn. As you were meant for me, he is not meant for you.

Tarragon knew sudden anger, and he growled low in his throat, his fingers closing over his palms into hard fists. He wanted to hit something. He shook his head and reeled in his emotions. Even he was surprised at the intensity of his feelings, how quickly it had risen. He had never been hot-headed before. What had changed?

He had changed. Into what, he didn't know.

It takes some getting used to, but we are now as one, and what you feel, I feel. What abilities I hold within me, you now have. I will teach you to control your emotions and your talent.

"What did you mean he is not meant for me? Brenn. Is. Mine. You have no right to—"

He is not the one meant for you. I am sorry, but it is the truth.

He. Is. Mine! Electricity rippled up and down Tarragon's arms and quickly converged over his fists. His eyes widened in surprise at how easily he had called on the forces. He had not even been aware he'd called them down. "What's happening to me?"

"Tarr?" Tarragon turned to the entrance of the cave, toward the softly spoken word.

Standing there was Brenn, a worried frown over his eyes. Even in the dim light of the moon, he could see the vibrancy of the violet eyes. There was worry in them, a concern that mimicked Tarragon's own.

He is not meant for you entreated Onik, his voice laced with love, concern, and regret.

I love him.

I feel your love for him. I feel his love for you. But he is not meant for you.

Stop saying that. Please. Tarragon sobbed in his mind. *I need him. I cannot lose him. I need him.*

Onik's presence began to fade. *I am sorry.*

"Tarr?" Brenn yelled as he ran toward him. "What's going on? I felt your pain. Are you all right? Did someone attack you?"

Tarragon lowered his head and allowed the electricity to simmer down. His hands were taken into warm ones. Beloved ones. He let out a sob and pushed them away, wrapping his arms around Brenn, then lowered his face into his neck.

"What is it? Tarr? What's happened?"

"I won't lose you," Tarragon sobbed. "You're mine."

Brenn stilled at his words, and he let out a sigh as he, too, wrapped his arms around Tarragon. For long moments, they stood under the light of the moon, amid the sounds of the night critters. A waft of fragrance rose in the air, calming both of them.

"I know I am not meant for you, Tarr. I told you this."

"No." Tarragon shook his head, not lifting it from Brenn's neck.

"You and I know you are meant for something greater, Tarr."

"No," Tarragon said again.

"Yes." Even though Brenn's voice was low, it was still insistent, and for some reason, that made Tarragon frightened. "You are now as one with a being we don't know anything about."

"I will never let you go."

Brenn sighed. It sounded full of regret. "You may have to find the strength to do just that."

"I love you, Brenn."

"I love you, too."

"I will never let you go."

Brenn didn't respond. Instead, he lowered his arms from Tarragon and stepped away. He raised his hand and cupped Tarragon's cheek.

"One of the hardest lessons I learned as I was being trained to control my magic was that I had to make hard decisions on life. I will have to teach you that. Are you ready?"

He has to be.

164

Onik's voice didn't whisper. It didn't come from inside Tarragon's mind. It came out of his mouth, and it was frightening.

"Who are you?" Brenn asked, surprise making his eyes widen, but he didn't step away.

I am Onik.

"When I am gone, please take care of my king. He is all I will ever have. All I will ever love."

I promise you that, Guardian.

Brenn lowered his head, and his tears fell to the ground. "Thank you."

And there is another thing I promise you, Guardian.

"One other? What would that be?"

I will make sure he heeds your call.

And then Onik's voice faded, and Tarragon could not summon him back. The tears dried in his eyes, and he looked up and met Brenn's gaze.

"Come," Brenn said, and Tarragon nodded, unable to speak, unable to process what had just been revealed.

"I may not be the one meant for you, sire, but Goddess, I am going to make sure I am *never* forgotten." With a smile on his face, a smile that warred between happiness and utter desolation, he took Tarragon's hand in his and led him back to the cave. There was nothing Tarragon could do or say. There was nothing he wanted to do or say but follow his beloved Guardian.

YOU MAY ALSO ENJOY THE FOLLOWING FROM EXTASY BOOKS INC:

The Hunt
Jo Tannah

Excerpt

"Welcome to Terrus, Master Kildud. My Lord Fulsam sent us to escort you to Castle Brock. He has been ill. Otherwise he would have come to meet you himself. He's been anxiously awaiting the arrival of you and your men since you sent confirmation you were coming in today."

"And you are?"

"Oh, I apologize." The man's cheeks reddened. "I'm Aldin, Lord Fulsam's personal secretary. My companions are called Fenton and Wesley. They are my assistants. I . . . uhm . . . I was the one who sent you that message." His voice trailed off to a whisper. The two men standing behind him bowed their heads at their introduction. They looked just as nervous and scared as Aldin. "If you and your men would follow us, we can take you to the transporters that will take us to the castle."

"Lead the way."

When Aldin hesitated once more, Marcus flashed him a toothy grin. Bruga stepped up beside Marcus. On his periphery, the rest of his men moved as one to flank their sides. Marcus wasn't surprised to see Aldin's fear return. After seeing that same expression for more years than he could count, he was used to it. His crew of merry men never failed to put the fear of the Goddess into those who saw them for the first time. Their sizes and heights plus the tattoos and weapons displayed out in the open were impossible to ignore. That they moved on silent feet for all their size and bulk only added to their menacing presence. Knowing his men, they would be doing the same thing he was—grinning broadly, puffing up their chests, and not concealing their curiosity. They exuded a confidence that was almost palpable.

Aldin's face went even paler, but he put on a smile before turning his back on them. He and his assistants looked at each other in silent communication before turning around as one to lead the way. The path they chose was paved and wound between the tall trees.

"They're very short." Although Bruga's face was devoid of expression, Marcus knew him well enough to hear the laughter in his voice.

"Don't be mean. Everyone's short next to you." Marcus turned and walked back to the cruiser. "Come on, let's get this program rolling. I don't like all this green." He added the last part under his breath.

"You've never liked green," Bruga said as he stepped up beside Marcus. "And you're not that short compared to me."

"It's just so . . . everything's so green. Can you imagine what crawls underneath all that foliage?" Marcus shivered when he felt his spine crawl and deliberately turned his back on the greenery.

"I know, I know. So. Come on, boss man. Best not keep our host waiting," Malik said. He'd obviously been standing behind him and Bruga. Marcus narrowed his eyes but chose not to acknowledge the young man's flippancy.

It didn't take long for them to finish loading their equipment and belongings into the three transporters standing by.

Soon they were on their way. Despite the thick vegetation, the road they were traveling on was clear and paved smooth. He leaned forward, taking in the details of his surroundings, not missing the way the roads curved around growths. It was as though whoever had designed them made sure to avoid the trees. Marcus turned to Aldin and saw the knowing look. Before he could voice his question, Aldin held up a hand and waved it toward the passing view.

"When my Lord's family first settled on this planet, they didn't wish for the environment to suffer damage from industrialization." It sounded as if Aldin had read his mind.

"I take it that the particular ancestor was an environmentalist?"

"Well, no, far from it. He was an industrialist."

Marcus frowned. "What happened to make him change his stance?"

"Sarit happened."

"Ah, yes. Sarit." Aldin was far from exaggerating his planet's economic wealth.

"The first lord made it illegal for any trees or natural habitats to be struck down to make way for roads and cities. As I think you've noticed, there are no straight roads on Terrus. Much of our infrastructure is constructed the same way." Aldin continued.

"Respect for the Goddess?" The question came from Bruga.

"Partly. On Terrus, we respect all of the Goddess' creations. Of course, if there is no other way around nature, we make sure to relocate whatever is affected to a safer place."

"Isn't that a bit expensive?" someone sitting at the back said. Marcus turned and saw that it had been Cody, one of his weapons analysts, who had spoken up.

"Money is irrelevant when it comes to respecting the Goddess' creations," Aldin said, almost serenely.

Marcus wondered how much, or how deeply, religion played a role in the people's culture.

Listening in on the conversation around him, Marcus wondered for the hundredth time why the Prelate needed their services. He and his men were nothing more than rangers for hire. The briefing provided to them did little to reveal anything critical that would have warranted emergency action or required their expertise. The information included focused only on Terrus' historical background and the staggering amount their team was to receive as compensation.

Marcus looked outside the transporter window while Aldin answered his men's questions. An unexpected, unwelcome sense of trepidation washed over him. There was nothing out there but greenery and wilderness. The shadows of the forest beyond the roads revealed unknown mystery and danger.

What had he gotten himself and his men into?

COMING SOON

Vol. II: Rise of the Symbionts

Technomage Wars Book 1: The Champion

GLOSSARY

Bobik: A dragon from the planet Nigul. Displays unmeasured and mysterious emphatic and magical abilities. He survives in a symbiotic relationship with Prince Kallen.

Dornijan dragon: Dragon of legend. Extinct race that once roamed Oryon.

Hobik: race of dragon symbiont that used to inhabit Nigul.

Indigo Artificial Brain or IAB: An intelligent, creative and self-aware machine. Tanis — controlled by Lando Garr. Gifted to Lando by Prince Kallen on Lando's twenty second birthday

Level 1A Security: Top Level genetically bred men and women whose main purpose is to protect high profile and very important individuals. Skill Level 1A of 20B, 1 being highest and twenty the lowest.

Lord Commander Militant: Highest rank of the military awarded to a trusted Level 1A Security.

Mage: learned men and women who practiced the arts of magic. Scorned by society, they are said to hide deep within the caverns of the Orana mountain range. They are feared by non-mages for their talents are strong and are long-lived.

Nigul: Not much is known about its former inhabitants, the Hobiks and their partners, for they all perished when the planet was destroyed by an asteroid. Home planet of Bobik.

Oryon: Home planet to the technomage royal family, Dacron. Current king, Arzhur Dacron.

Razboi: Fanatic militant group from the ultra-conservative planet, Verrphor. Distinctive clothes are flowing red robes with black masks.

Septurecce: A six-legged horse domesticated on Oryon.

Space conduit: Magical space portal allowing safe space travel on real time. Can only be opened by technomages.

Technomage: A rare occurrence within the ruling royal family of Oryon easily distinguishable by their violet colored eyes. Natural-born magicians who display an affiliation to anything technological and mechanical. There are currently four members of the royal family who display this ability: King Arzhur Dacron, Prince Kallen Dacron, Duke Eldron Zaruthra and Duke Drummond Caprici.

Psychem: Psychic with affiliation to body chemistry.

Vespa: Home planet to some of the known universe's best universities.

ALSO FROM JO TANNAH

Compelled, Winter Roses, Grass Stains and Flip Flops, Around The Block

Tales from the Archipelago: Kilig, The Secrets He Keeps

Taboo Series: Taboo, A Taboo Christmas, Taboo Pleasures, Christmas Unwrapped, The Summer Knows

Hidden Series: Hidden Evils, Hidden Dimensions, Hidden Fates

Rise of the Symbionts: Royal Guardian, Royal Consort, Royal Symbionts

Chronicles of the Serai: Heart Held Hostage

The Phantom Hunters: Waylaid

With Ann Mickan: Lemonade Stand, A Lemon Flavoured Christmas

Free Stories: Sock It To Me, Tell Him

ABOUT THE AUTHOR

I grew up listening to folk tales my father and nannies told either to entertain us children or to send home a message. These narratives I kept with me, and finally, I wrote them down in a journal way back when I kept one. Going through junk led to a long-forgotten box, and in it was the journal. Reading the stories of romance, science fiction and horror I had taken the time to put to paper brought to light that these were tales I had never met in my readings.

The tales I write are fictional, but all of them are based on what I grew up with and still dream about. That they have an M/M twist is simply for my pleasure. And I hope, yours as well.

Twitter: @JoTannah
Facebook Author Page: https://www.facebook.com/jotannahauthor
Website: http://jotannah.com
Email: jotannah1@gmail.com